ABOUT THE AUTHOR

Misha Gerrick lives near Cape Town, South Africa, and can usually be found staring at her surroundings while figuring out her next book.

She also spends a bit of time on mishagerrick.tumblr.com, and is looking forward to hearing from you.

I0621475

Also by Misha Gerrick

As Misha Gerrick

Anthology Short Stories:
Red Earth and White Light
In *Twisted Earths*
Chaos. Love. Hope.
In *Mayhem in the Air*
Ryan
In *The Thing that Turned Me* and *Ghosts of Fire*

As M Gerrick

The War of Six Crowns Series:
The Vanished Knight
The Heir's Choice

ENDLESS

Published by Five Muses Press, 2016
Cape Town, Western Cape, South Africa

This is a work of fiction. Any similarity between the characters and situations within its pages and places or persons, living or dead, is unintentional and co-incidental.

Cover photography from Adobe Stock

Cover and interior design by Misha Gericke

ENDLESS

MISHA GERRICK

DEDICATION

For Theresa.
You listened to me hash out the basis of this story, and said you'd get
your share of the royalties later.
Still not happening, but here's a special dedication instead.

ALERIA

This had to be what dying felt like. Floating outside my body, waiting for that final link to my life to be severed, only vaguely aware of indescribable pain. More screams than I could count rose up around me. Hundreds of footsteps beat against tiles. I couldn't open my eyes if I wanted to. Not when it was easier to listen and wait. People shouted for a doctor or an IV, or a thousand other things that made no sense. I listened to all the chaos, trying to untangle it in my thoughts.

Soon, I could go. The peace around me was so relaxing, completely out of place in the clamor I heard. I wanted it. To rest forever in that peace. Why not? There was a very good reason, but I couldn't call it to mind.

A numb buzz shot through my body and shattered my serenity.

It happened again. Only this time was more of a sharp pulse. The third time jolted like lightning. The fourth…Hell. Suddenly, the screams were coming from me. My heart's relentless thundering added to my torment.

Pain.

Everywhere.

My chest burned like fire. It hurt to breathe. Cold air drove down my throat and into my lungs, amplifying the

9

inferno in my chest. My skin felt scorched. It couldn't be. It wasn't right.

I had to see. I had to understand why pain dominated my existence like this. My eyes were fused shut. My breaths grew shallow, trying to draw air when there was none. I tried to clench my teeth. I bit hard plastic. A pipe. Cold air suddenly forced back into my lungs, out of time with my own breathing. This was wrong. It wasn't safe. I had to see. The best I got was a little fluttering of my lashes.

A high-pitched beep shot through my head. It repeated again and again. I wanted to reach over and slam my fist into its source. My arm wouldn't lift. Something kept it trapped. A scream rose up from the depths of my soul, but the pipe jammed inside my throat stifled the sound. I only managed a whimper, trying my best not to gag. More air blasted into my lungs against my will. What was going on? I was trapped in my own body, but why?

I needed to move. I had to move. Now. Before… Even… Even though… Panic gripped me. The beeps increased at a frenetic pace. *I needed to move.* To be gone. Didn't matter where. Just not here. Not defenseless. Not trapped.

The air sucked out of my lungs. I gasped, choking on nothing, strangled by invisible fingers. I tried to convulse my body. To twist myself free of what's holding me.

Nothing.

The air rushed back in a cold flood. Seconds later it left, only to return in the same amount of time.

There was a rhythm to the air. In… out… in… out… The breaths were slow—sleep-like. I concentrated on this rhythm, striving to clear my head. If I wanted out, I needed to think. Calmly. Clearly. Eventually, those irritating beeps slowed. I tried to focus past the sound.

Voices buzzed about me, adding to my need to see, to do something to protect myself. No one seemed to pay attention to me. Good. I could use that to my advantage.

I centered my every thought on moving my little finger. It finally jerked, but collided against something solid. So the thing trapping my arm was physical and too heavy for me to lift. It was better to be trapped than paralyzed. With luck I could escape my restraints. I tried my other hand, but it was cemented stuck as well. Right leg. Left leg. Damn it! Both trapped. I had to move!

No.

No, I needed to stay calm. I tried to make larger movements, biting the pipe in my mouth against the urge to scream in pain. There was no wiggle room.

Fearing that I might be blindfolded, I focused on blinking. It worked. My eyes opened and the blur faded, revealing ceiling tiles. Why would there be tiles? Where was the canvas of hospital tents? The distant sounds of bombs dropping? The power of their explosions rushing through my blood?

No. That wasn't right. I wasn't there.

Where was I, then?

I blinked again. My stinging eyes teared up and the moisture stung its way down my temples.

The buzzing conversation stopped.

My gag reflex kicked in, choking me in a futile attempt to cough out the pipe lodged in my throat. I tried to sit up and get my hands to my mouth. By some miracle, it worked, but whatever they were encased in knocked against plastic covering my mouth and pushed the pipe deeper down. More tears ran down my face.

Someone pushed my shoulders back into my mattress. "You need to calm down," a deep voice commanded.

Calm? *Calm?* This thing was making me choke! I wanted to rail at him, but my mouth had no free space to push the words out. My eyes rolled up as I fought for air.

"Relax," the voice repeated. "It's just your breathing apparatus. I can see you're able to breathe on your own, but we need to clear the carbon dioxide out of your body first."

Oh. Why didn't he say so? I was plugged into something forcing me to breathe and he acted as if it was a minor technicality. Idiot. My eyes turned back, focusing on a young man in a white jacket. This was my doctor?

Tired green eyes met my gaze. "Blink if you understand."

I blinked despite the fact that my lungs begged to be left alone.

"Good." He turned his mouth into something resembling a reassuring smile. "I can put you under again, if you're uncomfortable. Would you prefer that? Blink once for yes, twice for no."

No. No way was I going to be knocked out. I needed to move. I blinked twice.

"Approximate age: Twenty-five," a woman standing by my hip murmured. "She seems to be in excellent physical condition. Identifiable marks: a scar on right lower abdomen."

The doctor's head rounded towards her. "What?"

Unable to bend my neck, I turned my eyes to the woman. She was broad. Pale. Confused looking, with deep furrows etched between her brows.

"Yes," she said. "Whatever caused it must have gone right through. I'll go see if anyone is asking about a woman with a scar matching this one."

"No. I'll do it," the doctor said, taking the file from her. "You have a lot of work to do and I'm about to go on break."

The woman smiled. "You? Take a break? You'd better. You work too hard. I'll be checking on the other victims on my list."

Victims? She saw me as a victim? The word needled me in ways I couldn't begin to explain. That and her pitying smile before leaving me alone with the doctor. He regarded me again, a deep frown on his face. *What?* I wanted to scream at him again. *What!*

"Blink once for yes. Blink twice for no." He moved close, leaning over me. "Do you understand?"

I blinked once.

"Do I know you?"

The question stumped me. My heart rate picked up, increasing the frequency of the irritating beeps. I blinked twice.

He released a little sigh, hanging his head for a moment. "I'm Dr. Ryan."

Ryan… Ryan… Irish by name, but not by accent. In fact, his accent fell strangely on my ear. It was unlike anything I could remember. The beeps picked up speed to match my frantic heart.

"You're one lucky lady." His gaze flicked towards the machine, then back down. "Are you feeling okay?"

I blinked twice, trying not cry. He pulled a penlight from his breast pocket and shone it into both of my eyes. I winced and tried to turn my head.

"Do you remember what happened?" he asked, frowning.

I blinked twice, this time failing to keep the tears back.

The question shook me to the core. I couldn't remember anything. I tried to call up my name, my home, the date, anything. *Anything.* My memories didn't come. It was as if someone had locked me out of my own mind. My breathing sped up again and I couldn't stop it. The lack of air blurred my sight. I choked for air, stabbing pains through my torso. I was in trouble. Big. Huge trouble.

"Shhh, it's okay." Dr. Ryan moved out of my field of vision. A few seconds later, my soul floated again. He'd killed me. He must have. The deathly serenity trying to pull my soul from my body returned. A shudder raced over me as Ryan helped me lay back. This was what it felt like to die in my killer's arms.

RYAN

I waited for the patient to sleep before grabbing her stats. Once I was outside her cubicle, I made sure no one noticed me. Everyone was either absorbed in pain or horror, or busy trying to help.

My hands trembled as I flipped the file open. I took a hard look at the information. Nothing indicated anything out of the ordinary. At least, not for an airplane crash. Strange things happened in plane crashes. People who should have died, survived. People who, by all standards and odds, should have survived, died. Randomness in life made perfect sense. I knew this. I lived it. But this particular bit of randomness was dizzying.

That scar on her abdomen...

It couldn't be her.

If it was, why didn't she give me the same secret smile she'd sent me in wartime London, the day we walked away from each other, somehow—impossibly—friends?

If it was her, she'd smile and say, "You became a doctor? I can't believe it!"

Maybe. I never technically knew her. I'd hunted her, yes. For centuries.

The nurse had drawn the outline of the scar, and it matched the one I had a bit higher up my torso. A ragged I-shape. She had to be Aleria.

No, it couldn't be. Phoenix protectors regenerated. They manipulated fire and it couldn't harm them. Not unless someone like me had been actively stealing her life force. This woman was practically a crisp. On the other hand, crisps didn't wake up from induced comas so fast.

I glanced towards her curtained cubicle, running my fingers over scarred teeth marks in the flesh of my thumb. It had to be her. Instinct didn't buy into my rationale that it wasn't.

The suspicion was enough to send an almighty thrill through me. I curled my hands into fists and willed the feeling away. The creature behind that thrill was locked up in the darkest depths of my soul. Forever. It would stay that way, thanks to the woman who could be behind that curtain.

Could she really have changed my life without remembering?

No. It couldn't be her.

I shook my head and snuck off to give myself a morphine injection. Better to be safe.

NICK

Damn, I needed a smoke. My lungs burned to light up, but people frowned on it these days. For good reason, yeah. I just didn't care about those. Right now, I needed a smoke more than I needed to not have someone in my face about it. I shoved aside the witness testimonies on my desk and lit a cigarette. The first inhalation went down as smooth as good vodka. Romano scowled at me and leaned his hips against his desk.

"Do you really need to kill yourself like that?"

Yes. Other than having another griffon kill me—not a good idea—smoking was the best way I could think of to speed up my demise. Not that I could say so to Romano. If I mentioned my real name and age he'd have me institutionalized. It would be a disaster of epic proportions. I'd either have to escape and have the Firm track me down, or I'd have to phone them to break me out. Both options sucked. Better off not having people realize I hadn't aged for centuries.

I closed my eyes and took another long drag. "Craving, are we?"

"No. My former partner got me to kick the habit ages ago."

I grinned. "Then I don't see why this bothers you."

"Because I don't want to watch you die too." Romano

sent me an I'm-so-not-in-the-mood glare and dug into his pile of statements from air crash survivors. His partner had been killed when one of the Twin Towers collapsed. No possible terrorism case we ever had to investigate ever removed his survivor's guilt. This crash...it hit too close to home for him.

His eyes shot from side to side as he read. "Interesting. This one says two guys jumped up and prepared to C4 the cockpit when a woman in first class got up and kicked their ass."

"A woman?" That really made my day, knowing two terrorists had their asses handed to them by a girl. "Did she make it? I want to buy her some flowers."

Romano cracked a grin. Much better. "Good idea. Although it's unlikely she survived the explosion and the crash if she wasn't strapped in. Still, I'd like to know her name. She deserves a medal or something." He rifled through more statements. "A few witnesses say she was seated on 8C."

Good. I searched for the passenger manifest and brought up the name. Aleria Tyson. My heart thudded to a complete stop. Oh... Fuck. I inched my fingers to the cigarette pack and took out another, lighting it with the previous one's cherry. By some miracle, I managed not to shake. Romano lifted an eyebrow in question anyway.

I let my breath fan out slowly, calming myself down. It didn't have to be *the* Aleria. And thank God for that. It'd be hard going to explain how I had a five hundred year history with someone. Still, *that* Aleria was kick-ass too. But what would she be doing in the U.S.? As far as I knew, phoenix protectors centered around Britain unless they were on assignment. They also never traveled alone, so if it was her on the plane, there would have been three of them and the terrorists would have been fucked.

"Nothing. Her name's Aleria."

Romano nodded and rounded his desk. "Let's go give our plane's guardian angel a face." He bashed some keys with his forefingers, calling up her I.D. photo. He whistled. "Our girl's a hot one. British."

I sucked in way too much smoke. My eyes watered while I fought not to cough.

"British Hottie," I said, reverting to form out of habit. Nothing to do but look. It couldn't be her, but it would kill me not to know. So I rolled my chair over and rotated his screen to see.

And fuck. I needed a third cigarette. Long, straight, golden-brown hair. Serious blue eyes that sparkled like a frozen lake when she laughed. Beautiful mouth; wide enough, full enough. Perfect, really. I couldn't stop staring if I wanted to. In fact, I didn't want to. It *was* her. My Poison. *Alya.* She was an addiction I'd gone cold turkey on. I'd spent the past two hundred years trying not to think about her, and now she was smack bang in the middle of my case.

Romano turned the screen back and typed some more. "Always did like them classy."

My gaze flitted to my crumpled pack of cigarettes. Why was she here? I couldn't face her again. Not ever. Griffons and phoenixes tended not to get along. The two of us used to be an exception. Then I fucked up. Now she'd probably kill me. She'd be right to. Because she *was* alive. Another thing about protectors: They didn't die easily. Not even with a griffon around to suck out their life force. She was out there somewhere. We'd meet again.

We'd have to act like we never met before.

"She's unaccounted for," Romano said, sighing softly. "Fuck, I hate those bastards."

We all hated terrorists. The FBI. Our task team investigating the plane crash, Romano in particular. I lightly patted his shoulder. Part of me yearned to go find Alya. A stupid, stupid idea. A stupid, *necessary* idea. She was an important part to the puzzle. Only she had gotten close enough to I.D. the two terrorists. With her help, we could nail whoever was responsible, because for some reason, none of the terrorist organizations we knew were claiming responsibility.

I was so screwed.

ALERIA

I was a little girl running from monsters. The worst sort of monsters, who spoke and looked like me, but older. They ran like me, but faster.

They wanted to kill me.

Yellow light bathed the coarse tree trunks surrounding us and showed me the way I should run. Crashing footsteps crumbled leaves and snapped twigs, growing louder with each passing moment. I wasn't running fast enough. I was too small. My long dress tangled around my legs. Would it hurt to die?

Again and again, their baying voices told me how close they were.

"We have her!" one shouted in French, but with a strange accent. They whooped like dogs snapping at my ankles. I hiked my dress up higher, cursing my mother for insisting I wear it in the first place.

A crash to my left drew my attention. A man broke through the undergrowth to catch me. His torch doused me in yellow light before I veered to the right. I could only hope they'd lose me. I needed to find somewhere to hide, but how would I keep them out? They'd definitely find me. These monsters never failed.

My sides ached. My feet throbbed from stumbling over roots. I couldn't stop. I pushed my body harder, driving myself through branches and foliage. They were coming in from my right. It would only be a matter of time before they hemmed me in. Flickering shadows danced to my left. My own shadow shivered among them, moving with the wind caused by the monsters' motions.

The shadows suddenly tore on a bramble bush. I skidded to a halt. Someone released a victorious laugh behind me, but the sight gave me a flicker of hope. I knew these vines. Luc and I often crawled into them to pick the sweetest berries.

Heart thudding, I dove into the thorns, crying out when they bit into my flesh. They tangled with my hair, tore at my dress. My mother took weeks to make it and now it'd be ruined beyond repair. Each tear to the skirt freed my movements a little more, giving me a chance at survival. The monsters didn't want to kill me here. If they did, they could have done it ages ago.

I kept crawling deeper into the brambles, stopping only briefly to free my hair. A few feet later I fell into a hollow. The monsters cursed behind me. I whimpered and collected my tattered skirt about me as I pressed back against the hollow's wall. Blood trickled over my skin in too many places to count. I was alive, but I was still as good as dead. They could wait me out. I'd starve or die of cold before surrendering.

One of the monsters dropped to his knees and held his torch to the brambles' edge. I was doused with blinding light. I couldn't even make out a face.

"I can see her," the one with the strange accent said. His hand shot through the brambles and grasped my ankle.

I screamed and grabbed the branches behind me,

heedless of the thorns tearing into my palms. He yanked me so hard I lost my hold and dragged me farther and farther from safety. Out of desperation, I bent over and bit his hand as hard as I could. His bitter blood flooded into my mouth.

The monster cried out in pained surprise, jerking his hand away from me. "The brat bit me!"

I was about to spit out his blood when another asked, voice tensed, "Did she swallow any of it?"

Swallow? Disgusting! Yet the panic in the monster's voice made me think twice. The one with the odd accent knelt close again, just in time to see me take a big breath and gulp the blood down.

"Shit! She did." Strange accent dove in after me, screaming as the brambles caught him mere inches away. With a frustrated roar, he bore down towards me, but his larger size slowed him down.

I carefully crawled deeper into the brambles. I heard laughter behind me.

"Oh look. Ryan—outwitted by a child."

Ryan cursed and continued to struggle, making the branches about me shiver. I crawled deeper in. Sweat sheened my body. My stomach roiled. Trembles wracked me.

I kept going, even though I felt weaker with every passing moment. I lost awareness of their voices, focusing in on one thing. Dad. I had to get to my dad. He was safety. I kept crawling as stealthily as I could until I found the tunnel Luc and I had made to pick the berries. I crawled out and kept crawling until everything but the sound of my thundering heart died away.

I fought against the weights restraining my limbs, struggling to sit up. Hands pinned me down, then turned on the light.

Ryan.

I screamed, crying while cowering back against the mattress. Instead of attacking me, Ryan stepped back, his green eyes wide.

"I'm not going to hurt you," he whispered, glancing behind him. "It was a nightmare."

Nightmare? My monitor's fast beeps filled the silence between us. Nightmare… I forced myself to relax, letting my body sag back into the mattress. The air machine did my breathing for me.

Seriously, how could I think it was real? Ryan was my doctor and the dream had some stupid fantasy of 1400s France or something. I glanced towards him with an apologetic expression. His posture eased, as if he'd held his breath until now. He moved closer and checked my vitals.

"Looking good," he murmured. "Bet you want that thing out of your mouth."

I blinked. I'd have nodded if I could. Vigorously.

He smiled gently. Nothing like the monster of my dream. "Okay, good. I'm going to take it out for you and we'll talk. Just stay calm. This might make you feel a bit sick. Now exhale and I'll take out the tube."

I blinked again and did as he said. He started to remove the pipe. Sure enough, my stomach crawled its way up my throat. Moments later, the pipe was out. I took deep breaths as fast as I could, partly to savor my freedom from that damned machine and partly to keep my nausea at bay. My throat ached.

"Well done." He held a glass of water close to my mouth, helping me get a hold on the straw. I sucked greedily. The icy coolness was heaven, but it hurt to swallow. "Now," he said, placing the glass on a table by my bed. "What's your name?"

It would have been wonderful if we could have started off with something a little more comforting.

"I don't know." My voice sounded brittle.

He paused. "Do you know why you're here?"

"No," I croaked. I longed for more water.

Ryan frowned and returned to my side, flashing a light into my eyes. I flinched at the reminder of my dream. My heart rate rose again.

"We'll need to do a scan," he said, turning the penlight off. He glanced to the heart monitor.

I swallowed. "You. Nightmare." It hurt too much to speak.

"I was in the nightmare?"

"Yes." I coughed, prompting him to give me more water.

"What did you dream?"

There was no way in hell I'd tell him the whole thing. First, it was ridiculous. Second, my throat felt like I'd eaten sandpaper. I rolled my eyes and croaked the keywords. "Torches…monsters…brambles…you… I bit…you. Stupid…dream."

Ryan replaced the cup once more. "I see. Do you remember anything else? Maybe we can figure out who you are."

Something about his measured response set me on

edge. "Nothing."

He frowned. He didn't believe me.

"Nothing," I repeated, emphasizing both syllables. The effort shredded my poor throat.

Ryan took a notebook from his coat's pocket and scribbled. My gaze drifted to his hand. It had a faint scar. Teeth marks. My jaw dropped, but no scream came. Pure terror took over my body. My body jerked up, but he dropped the notebook and forced me to lay back. He covered my mouth with his hand to stifle my screams.

"Quiet!"

Quiet? Quiet? His hand. His scar. No, wait. Maybe I saw it before without realizing.

"I'm way past hurting you," he hissed, glancing towards the curtained entry. His words shattered any illusion I had. The nightmare was real. The danger too.

I shivered and closed my eyes, letting my soul reach out... For what?

"Don't. I want to help you," he said, "but you need to trust me."

I wanted to bite his hand, but if my nightmare was right, it wasn't a good idea. I gave a little nip instead and he yanked his hand back.

"*Trust?*" I hissed back. "You wanted to *kill me.*"

"Hundreds of years ago, yes!" He sighed and wiped his hand down his face. "You need to rest. You really remember nothing?"

"NO!"

"Okay! Shit. Shit. *Shit.*" He paced about, then stopped and faced me once more. "The FBI will want to talk to you tomorrow. Do *not* mention the fact that you're six centuries old. I'll make sure the hospital system spits you out." He gave me a look over. "And…ensure no one notices how fast you're healing."

FBI? I was in America? I was six hundred years old? I didn't feel like I had six centuries behind me. Bloody hell that was a lot of memory I didn't have. Wait. "Spit me out where? I don't know where to go."

Ryan scowled. "Nor do I know where you're supposed to be. But you need out of the hospital."

"Or what?" I asked, narrowing my eyes.

"Or humans will realize you're immortal. And then we're all screwed."

ALERIA

I sipped at the water Ryan held to my mouth, eyeing him nervously. His face showed me very little of his thoughts, which worried me. I glimpsed the scar on his hand as he set the glass aside.

"I know this is difficult for you," he said softly, "but you really need to trust me. You can't tell them anything."

Them. The FBI. I was pretty sure lying to them was a serious offence. At the same time, I couldn't shake the feeling that this wasn't the first time I lied about who—or what—I was. Not remembering anything was a disaster in the making. How would I know if I made a misstep?

"I know," I said, briefly closing my eyes. "I do trust you." That much was true. I just didn't know if it was wise to do so.

He leaned over and rewarded me with a smile, which completely transformed his face. His eyes lightened to the same green as the ocean. And…well…he seemed much less intimidating. "Good. I'll be right here, okay?"

I nodded. A short while later, the curtains swished open and two men entered. I instinctively knew both were packing. Other than that, they had nothing in common when it came to looks. One was swarthy, Italian looking. His black hair was cropped close, making his features seem sharper. His dark eyes flicked to Ryan. "Doctor, I'm sure you have work to do."

His blond partner's piercing blue gaze shot to Ryan as well. His step faltered before a shocked look came my way. A thrill of recognition buzzed through me. I knew this man. Somewhere. Somehow. I wanted to reach out and touch his cheek. I wanted to ask why he looked so tired and unkempt. He cleared his throat and glanced away.

I frowned. "I prefer Dr. Ryan to stay here, if that's okay. I–it's been disorienting."

The swarthy one came towards my bedside. "Of course. I'm Agent Dean Romano. This is my partner, Agent Nick Parker." I glanced Agent Parker's way, but he was busy staring at Ryan, who leaned back against the only wall in my cubicle. Something about this was off. Ryan's studied nonchalance didn't ring true and Nick Parker's name only rang a vague bell. Nothing like the reaction I'd felt when he came in.

Romano's glance followed mine. "You two know each other?"

The other two men broke eye-contact to meet Romano's gaze.

"Yeah." Parker half-smiled. "We went to the same school."

Ryan occupied himself by studying my stats, which I was convinced he knew by heart. After all, he'd forged them. "It's been a long time."

So they knew each other. And I knew Parker, the one who just wouldn't meet my gaze. Wait. School? What school? How did Ryan really know Parker? Was he immortal too?

Yes. The answer came to me as instinctively as breathing, but for some reason, I didn't feel even remotely threatened by him. Instead, I wanted to know why I knew Parker and why he seemed so…tired. I wanted like hell to know why I longed to reach out and soothe him.

Romano opened a notebook and took out a pen. "I know this will be difficult for you, but we need to talk about the plane crash."

"I…can't."

My words drew Parker's attention. "Can't?"

Damn, if only I could nod, but Ryan had insisted I keep the stupid neck brace on. The casts were still on too. As were the bandages to cover burn wounds I no longer had. "Sorry."

Parker frowned. "Why?"

This time it was my turn to avert my eyes. "I forgot."

"Forgot?" He moved into my field of vision. It triggered something. A bright flash of music and laughter and me panicking. I winced and closed my eyes.

"She has retrograde amnesia," Ryan said. "She only knows about the crash because I told her it happened. Nothing else. We're hoping it was the concussion she got, but it could be psychological. Please don't feed her details, she needs to remember on her own."

"Amnesia," Parker repeated dully, then he laughed. "I'm sorry, but I'm having trouble believing this."

It felt like someone pressed a hot bar behind my eyes. "Why?" I demanded. "Because it's inconvenient?"

Parker squinted at me, but Ryan forestalled him. "Ali, they need to ask."

"Ali?" Nick mouthed, frowning.

I scowled at him. "Fine." I purposefully focused my

attention on Romano. "I'm sorry, but I just can't remember anything."

"Nothing?"

Ryan passed him the real results from the psyche evaluation I went through yesterday. "Here. She can't even remember the year. She only knows her name because you linked her to the passenger manifest."

Romano paged through the file. "We were really hoping you could remember what the terrorists looked like. Two hundred people died and we want to bring those responsible to justice."

I shook my head. "I wish I could help."

"Hey." Romano gave me a gentle smile. "Maybe you'll remember something later. If you do, call me, okay?" He took a business card from his breast pocket and placed it on my table.

"Okay," I said, glancing at Nick as he placed his card on top of Romano's. If his frown went any deeper, it'd be carved into his face permanently.

"Ryan, can I talk to you alone?" he asked. As casual as his voice sounded, I didn't buy it. From the tension in Ryan's posture, neither did he. Ryan left the cubicle anyway.

NICK

Ryan led me to an office nearby and shut the door. The place was plain vanilla. Except for his diplomas on the wall behind the desk, nothing personal indicated that the medium sized office even belonged to him. Nothing gave a hint of the life he led, or the lives he took to keep living.

"Didn't think I'd see you again, Niko," Ryan said.

Yeah. That had been the plan. "What the fuck are you doing?"

He crossed his arms, eyeing me down his nose the way he used to. "I'm a doctor, now."

"What did you do? Disappoint Daddy?" I dropped into the visitor's chair and rested my feet on his desk.

Ryan's expression darkened. Bingo. "I'm rogue."

"The hell?" If he said he'd upped and married Aleria, I'd have been less surprised.

Going rogue meant kicking the absolute worst habit in existence: power addiction. It never really went away. Especially not when the griffon in question had spent centuries hunting phoenixes for their life forces. The longer we hunted, the harder it became to kick the addiction. Ryan was the second oldest griffon I knew.

"You," I said, recovering some of my cool. "That's not possible. You're the worst of us all."

Ryan rolled his eyes and went to his desk. He stacked

his papers carefully and slowly, buying time to figure out what to say. "I didn't say it was easy. Living on juice is a bitch."

Which explained why he became a doctor. Easy morphine source. Bastard. "What the fuck are you doing with Aleria?"

"Not your business."

"You know it's my business," I shot back, hands itching to deck him. The nicotine cravings didn't help either.

"Last I recall, she told you she'd rip out your spine if you came near her." He ran his hand across his stubbled jaw. "That's why—"

My eyes narrowed. "If you're doing this to kill her—"

"I'm not." Ryan's shoulders sagged and he swiped his hand up his face.

The surprises kept coming. "Really?"

His hand slowed to a halt in his hair. "I don't think."

Now I had to laugh. It was bitter, though. Dry. "Typical. Why don't I just put you out of your misery and leave it at that?"

He took the utmost care to lay the papers back onto his desk, but the stare he fixed on me told me all I needed to know. That the morphine kept only the barest traces of control over his killing instincts. That despite his having stopped hunting decades ago, he was still the single most powerful griffon in existence.

If I so much as twitched, he'd hand my ass back to me in three minutes tops. I wouldn't even have time to burn through my own morphine dosage before he kicked my ass. He'd have me before I drew my gun.

"Then why are you hanging around Aleria like a

vulture?" I asked, trying to figure out if potentially revealing my location to rogue-hunters was worth the joy of wringing Ryan's neck. Because the moment I didn't have morphine dulling my power, any un-medicated griffon in the area would be able to sense me.

Ryan's jaw set, but after a moment, he did answer me. "To protect her."

My face went slack. "Protect? You? Her?"

"She's alone, unguarded and one of the most vibrant phoenixes in existence. If someone in the Firm finds out she's vulnerable…"

She'd be as good as dead. Damn griff had a point, but it still didn't explain why he'd want to keep her safe.

"What brought the change of heart?" I demanded.

All I got was one of his empty stares. "Goodbye."

He moved past the desk and gestured toward the door.

That really pissed me off. Him ordering me around like I was still one of his side-kicks. Like I was still his baby brother. Like I could be dismissed at any moment just because he grew tired of my presence. I stood up, keeping my movements insolent and uncaring. He wasn't the guy I looked up to anymore. He couldn't awe me. Intimidate me, yes, but I'd never show it.

I smirked at him.

"Touchy, are we?" I asked, baiting him. If he was rogue, he couldn't do anything to me anyway. He prepared to speak, but I jumped right in again. "Too bad. I get the feeling you'll see me again real soon."

Ryan's glower went as dark as night during a blizzard, but someone knocked before he replied. The door opened and Dean popped his head inside. His keen gaze traveled from me to Ryan, then back to me. Great, I'd have tons of questions to deflect now.

"You ready to go?" he asked me.

Ryan's expression remained inscrutable, but I sensed a bit of smugness. He thought he had me under control.

"Yeah." I strode out. Out the office, out the hospital, out the lot. I walked to the end of the block and lit up, waiting for Dean to catch up. Let him kiss Ryan's ass. I wouldn't. I'd show Ryan exactly how uncontrollable I could be when I wanted. When it came to Aleria's safety, Ryan would have a tough time keeping me away.

NICK

Three days. Three days of knowing where *she* was and I'd turned into a wreck. It was ridiculous. Grumbling to myself in Russian, I slammed into my apartment. I lit up a smoke and took a long drag.

Poison.

From the first time I'd met her alone, I'd known she'd be the death of me. Did that keep me away? No. Of course not. I'd sought her out as if suddenly my addiction was to keep her alive and with me.

I rubbed my thumb over my brow, trying to decide on what to do next. Exhaustion weighed me down. Every work day reminded me of Alya. Especially with the press pushing to have her name revealed.

Then there was Romano, who was just a bit too sharp to buy my story of Ryan and me simply not getting along. He was pushing me for answers I couldn't give. After three days, I doubted he'd stop anytime soon.

A drink. I needed a drink.

Letting the cigarette hang from my lips, I trudged to the kitchen and poured myself a good measure of vodka. I downed it. Slowly, the thoughts buzzing in my skull like a million bees at least slowed slightly.

I took a moment to savor my cigarette, but the peace didn't last.

Alya alone in the hospital made me nervous. If she'd failed to shield her power, griffons would already be staking the place out to take her. Would Ryan be able to guard her all the time? No. He had duties. He couldn't stop taking morphine or the worst of the worst would find him. So if someone slipped past security, Alya might be dead by the time he checked up on her.

I couldn't let that happen.

I was half-way to the door before I made myself stop. If I showed up at the hospital, Alya would want to know why. Better if she didn't remember me. Better for her.

Better for me, too.

Her safety was more important. I'd find a way to keep watch at a distance.

"Stupid," I muttered and marched myself back to the kitchen for some more vodka. "She's shielding, you fool. If she wasn't, Ryan would already have had to deal with at least one griff coming to investigate."

Saying it out loud made me feel better. More like I was talking sense. I poured myself another drink. Strange, come to think of it. Ryan had kept both his names.

My cell went off, jarring me. Romano. I scowled and answered. "I'm not going out with you and Carla."

"She's dead."

Everything in me went cold. I couldn't breathe past the hollow ache settling in my chest.

"Who?" I forced out. I fucking knew who.

Romano sniffed, not deigning to answer the question. "A super-virus. Something *real* nasty, apparently." His sarcasm almost flew over my head. "Hey Parker, guess who signed the order for her immediate cremation?"

My grip on the phone tightened. "Ryan." If he killed

her, I didn't give a fuck. He was dead.

"Yup. Suspicious as hell." Papers rustled in the background. "I'm checking out the records. Can't put my finger on it, but something is wrong with your school friend."

Oh yeah, there will be. But first, I needed to talk Romano down. This line of inquiry would get him killed.

"Romano." I used my best patronizing tone. "Do you think he crashed the plane?"

The rustling stopped. "No."

"Okay… Do you think he killed her?"

Romano actually thought it over. I could practically hear him turning the question about in his mind. "No."

"Then what?"

"I dunno," he muttered, sighing. Then he chuckled. I pictured him pinching the bridge of his nose. "You're right."

I hated myself for doing this. "You said you're going to take the night off. Do it."

"I will. Good night."

"Night."

After disconnecting the call, I went to my room. I took my service pistol from its holster and swapped it with one that can't be traced back to me. I usually slept with it under my pillow. It was loaded with silver bullets for exactly this sort of situation.

Ryan could own me when it came to fighting griffon against griffon. Luckily for me, this was revenge. I had no interest in playing fair. As tempting as it was to burn through the morphine in my system and fly to the hospital, I restrained the impulse. Ryan had given in to his addiction. If I approached without morphine, he'd sense me long before I was there. Not a good idea.

I didn't mind dying. I *did* mind failing.

So I drove.

I arrived at the hospital. Went to the front desk. The receptionist smiled exactly right. Not too bright in case I was a family member of someone about to die. Not too somber in case I was someone about to receive good news.

"Dr. Ryan, please."

The receptionist typed away on her computer. "Sorry, sir, but he's not on duty at the moment."

I grimaced. "Dang. I'm sorry I missed him. Do you have a number I can call?"

Her perfect little smile faded. "I'm sorry, but we're not allowed to give out personal details."

"Of course," I said. "Was worth a shot. Have a good night."

Well, fuck. This was inconvenient. Did I power up and track him down? I made my way back out the front door, trying to decide, but then it struck me. He'd come back to the hospital eventually. Even if only to cover his tracks so he couldn't be found.

I'd just make sure to be here when he did.

RYAN

I sauntered in just as the hospital shift was about to change, hoping to attract as little attention as possible.

The receptionist beckoned me closer, a concerned frown drawing her brows together. "Dr. Ryan, someone came looking for you here in the dead of night."

Splendid. Unexpected people asking for me never boded well. "Did he leave a name?"

She shook her head. "Good looking guy. A bit scruffy looking. Blonde." Her nose wrinkled. "I think he smokes."

Ah. Nikolai. The only griffon I knew who was insane enough to smoke. Seemed like he was serious when he threatened me about Ali. He probably got news about her 'death'.

"Thanks," I said. "If you see him again before you go, tell him we'll be right out."

"We?"

"Me and his sister." I forced a parting smile I didn't feel like and headed to my office.

Irritation dogged my every step. What was his problem? He'd been the first one to go rogue between the two of us, but somehow he kept acting like I was the one who couldn't be trusted.

Unless this was specifically about Ali.

To whom I had given my office's key and instructions to lock herself in until morning.

Who might not be here anymore. If she didn't trust me, she could be out there alone without anyone to help her. Or maybe she remembered the monster I was.

I walked faster and tried the door as soon as I reached it. Still locked. I let out the breath I'd held and knocked. "It's me."

The door opened and Ali stepped back, slightly pale. She wore a t-shirt, pair of jeans, jacket, and cowboy hat. All items from the lost and found.

"You scared me when you didn't knock first," she said.

Stupid of me. I must have terrified her. "Sorry."

She shrugged, then tried for a tremulous smile. Somehow, she made it look good. "Are we going now?"

I nodded. "Let me get you a wheelchair."

The moment I wheeled Ali out of the hospital, she smiled and lifted her face to the sun. She basked in its warmth. Drew it into herself like a woman starved.

Even with my morphine dose set to maximum, my true nature sat up to take notice. It wanted to snuff out her life and draw it into me.

I was in trouble.

I forced my eyes away and gulped in deep breaths. She needed my help. I couldn't betray that. Not after she'd changed my life.

Somehow, the memory of that fateful day calmed down my inner monster, but also reminded me that I was far from the only danger to her. I kept wheeling her away from the hospital. The faster I got her away, the better.

The fact that records of her stay existed burned in the back of my mind. If I could have, I would have destroyed all of it, but it wasn't possible. She was a prime witness in a terrorism investigation. Someone would notice if she disappeared without a trace, so I had to make her die instead and hope to God that no griffon got around to sniffing through the paper trail I'd left. It had been a pain in the butt just to keep photographers from seeing her. The heroine of flight 598.

With her dead, nothing would keep her identity secret. Unless her kin the phoenixes stepped up and killed the story.

All hell would break loose if one of the big players recognized her, and they would. As soon as they saw her. She was every griffon's Holy Grail. Another thing for which I was to blame.

"Are you sure this is okay?" she asked.

I tightened my hold on the wheelchair's handles and met her gaze. "Of course."

"You just seem…conflicted."

"It's okay. I can handle it."

I could only hope.

"Oh, hey!" Nick exclaimed, stepping out from behind one of the hospital's pillars. He had a nerve to sound surprised. "I heard you died." He dropped a bouquet of roses into Ali's arms. Orange, rimmed with red. I scowled at him.

He should have left when he'd gotten the news that Ali was still with the living.

Ali checked my reaction first, then smiled at him. "Thank you!" She inhaled the roses' scent. "What are they for?"

Excellent question. After the FBI interview, she'd asked me if she knew Nick as soon as I'd walked into her cubicle. I couldn't be sure at the time, but from the way he wouldn't back off, it was a safe bet that she did.

"Nothing," Nick said, smiling. "We got off on the wrong foot and when I heard you died, I felt bad. Then Ryan let me know you didn't and I wanted to apologize." He wore his most charming smile.

I rolled my eyes. "Touching gesture. Good day, Agent Parker." I made to push her past him, but he fell in with us. His cocky swagger set my teeth on edge. "Don't you have a case you need to be working on?"

"Now that you mention it, I need to talk to Aleria and see if she remembers anything."

"Still nothing, I'm afraid," Ali said, hugging the roses a little closer.

Was that a hopeless sagging of shoulders I detected on Nick? He caught me watching and recovered almost instantly. "Are you sure? Because if you did, I'm sure Ryan would tell you I'd understand."

She glanced his way, brows furrowed. "You're like him, aren't you?"

"You do remember," he said.

"Only that I know you." Her eyes searched his face. Sure enough, there was something in his expression. Almost like hunger… Or lust…but not quite. Yearning

No. Fucking. Way. Clearly I'd need to have a little chat with Russian Boy.

"How?" she asked, turning toward him in her eagerness to know. "When did we meet?"

"Don't," I commanded, but I didn't need to. He'd paled as if she'd asked him to die. Obviously, he had as little desire as I did to talk about anything leading up to a specific point in our lives.

Aleria wrinkled her nose at me. "Ryan wants me to remember on my own."

Nick's expression eased. "I see. I heard somewhere that it's the best way."

"And yet, I'd prefer to know and be done with it."

"You would," Nick said and squeezed her shoulder. The gesture was completely natural. Thoughtless as if he was used to touching her.

Ali tilted her head towards his hand slightly, but stopped short of making contact.

Nick's hand dropped away. "How are you two getting home?"

"Taxi," I said, frowning at him.

"Nonsense." Nick objected. "I have my car here."

"It's okay."

"No, no," he said, sizing me up. "I insist."

Ali's keen gaze shot between us. "Please?"

Her simple request was like a little stab to where it hurt most, but damn, how could I say no? Besides, Nick seemed intent on protecting her, which could only be a good thing. Pain in the ass though he was, I still trusted him.

I sighed. "In that case, show us the way."

Nick led us to his car and opened the back door for Ali. She smiled up at him and slid into the seat with an easy grace no person could fake. Nick watched her, then prepared to close the door, but I moved fast and got in after her. He shut the door with a passive-aggressive little flourish and got in behind the wheel.

"Where to?" he asked while starting the car. I gave him my address and he whistled. "Fancy digs. But then, you probably would have run home for anything less than a five star hotel suite."

That was bullshit and he knew it. All this was to make me look like an idiot in front of Aleria. I leaned back in my seat and casually slipped my arm behind Ali's head. Just to get to him. To my surprise, Ali shifted a bit nearer as we drove. I smiled, oddly elated by the tiny movement.

Her face was turned outside to the many skyscrapers around us, but I watched her flashing reflection in the window. A mixture of confusion, bewilderment, and a generous dollop of fear appeared in her eyes. I took a chance and drew her to even closer to me, keeping my hand on her arm.

She accepted it. No. She smiled up at me and welcomed it. My true nature didn't like this one bit, but I didn't care. I smiled back and gave her arm a little rub. She slowly relaxed, resting against me while she gazed out over the passing buildings. This time, she seemed much calmer. She trusted me. Actually trusted me. Amazing.

Nick cleared his throat, snapping me out of my wonderment. "So…you'll be staying with Ryan?" He caught my eye in the rearview mirror, sending me a definite *back-off* glare.

"Yeah," Ali said. "Until I can get back on my feet."

"How kind," he said, not quite keeping the sarcasm out of his voice.

I fought the urge to kick the back of his seat. Instead, I took long, slow breaths and leaned back. Nothing good ever came from losing my temper.

"I think it is," Ali said. "I don't know how much more afraid I would have been if he hadn't found me out." Her defensiveness caught me off guard. "It was terrifying in the beginning."

Nick muttered something about her still needing to be afraid under his breath. If Ali heard him, she didn't show it.

We drove the rest of the way in not-quite comfortable silence. Ali stared up the side of my building in awe as we parked. It was impressive, glinting with glass and steel and reaching high into the sky like a tree trying to outgrow its neighbors. "It's huge."

"Wait until you see the inside," I said, smiling. "The view's stunning."

"Let me guess," Nick said, glancing up as well. "Penthouse."

"It's like you know me," I said and led them inside.

Nick followed us into the elevator. I sighed, but kept my peace. His being here was a good thing. If I kept telling myself so, maybe I could convince myself that it was true.

As soon as the elevator doors parted, I marched down the short hallway to the penthouse's door. I swiped my key-card through the lock and swung the door open for Ali to step in first. She gasped and went straight to one of the picture windows.

"Amazing," she breathed. "I love this place."

"It's okay."

She glanced over her shoulder and I shrugged. I always liked the apartment, but it took having people over to realize how cold it was. Neat, clean lines. Black, white, and red. Modern, sleek furniture to offset years spent amongst my father's antiques, arranged to make the best of the living room's space. The open-plan kitchen and dining area were to the left. The kitchen was spacious, the way I preferred, and the black dining table was big enough to seat four people. The windows were the real showpiece, stretching floor to ceiling and across the entire wall, giving me a panoramic view over Manhattan.

I used to like the order and space in the apartment. Now, with Ali here, it felt too clinical. I shrugged off my coat and went for hers.

She let me pull it off. "You must love the view most."

"I used to, but you get used to it after a while. I do like the sense of space, though. In the city—"

"But above everything," Nick cut in.

I didn't miss the verbal jab. If he thought I didn't realize how vulnerable protecting Ali made us all, he was wrong. There wasn't a better way. Not while she was unable to remember anything.

Ali yawned. "Mmm…don't know where that came from."

"You're healing. It'll be a few more days before you feel up to scratch. Let me take you to your room."

"I'll fall asleep," she warned.

"That's okay," Nick said. "Take a nap. We'll have a nice dinner ready by the time you're awake."

She smiled and let me show her the way to the guest room. It lacked personality. I never entertained, so I never bothered to add anything to the standard hotel-like décor the interior designer had gone with. A bed with a high, cushioned gray bed stile. Black bedside tables. Chrome lamps with black shades. Single Chinese characters painted on white and framed in black.

This didn't suit Ali. Still, she smiled and complimented my taste before flopping onto the bed with a contented sigh. "Heavenly."

I leaned against the doorjamb, watching her. "Let me

know if you need anything, okay?"

"Okay." She peeked up and met my gaze, smiling. "Ryan?"

"Yeah."

"Thanks."

I sent her a jaunty smile and a small bow before closing the door.

Nick had started cooking while I was with her. It was a skill all griffs learned early. With our metabolism being pretty damn fast, we got very hungry, and often. Still, seeing him there, making himself at home in my kitchen, brought a frown to my face. He wasn't supposed to be here. We'd stopped speaking decades ago.

"I don't think she'll wake up before tomorrow morning." The scent of frying onions wafted my way. My stomach made a little hungry twist.

"What the fuck are you thinking?" Nick demanded, eyeing me like I'd said I was about to die or something else insane.

"That the onions smell good." My stab at humor didn't go over well. I sighed. "I couldn't let her wander off alone."

He blinked. "You *couldn't*?"

"Oh, shut it. Believe it or not, I've changed." I picked up a knife and casually flicked it into position to cut the beef he'd taken out of the fridge.

"Griffs like you don't change. You said so yourself."

I busied myself with dicing the meat into blocks. Truth was, I'd tried to change. In the decades since the Second World War, I hadn't crossed the line to my true nature. Not once. Yet right now, my every fiber was honed in on Ali. It was all I could do not to break through the bonds I used to keep my true nature in check.

"Could be I was wrong," I said.

Nick cut up some vegetables with efficiency born out of centuries of practice with a knife. He kept his obvious doubts to himself.

"I'm low," he said after a while. "Do you have stock?"

Telling him to go get his own morphine was an excellent way to get rid of him, but something held me back. Maybe it was our old friendship, or because he hadn't taken the argument further—as if he wanted to believe me.

I nodded. "There's a fridge in my safe. In my room. Combination's 150400."

Nick smirked and put down his knife. "You mystery, you."

I rolled my eyes. It was a mystery. The people who knew where I lived, but had no idea what I was, would never guess my true birthdate—15 April 1000—let alone that it was my safe's combination. Those who could guess didn't know where I lived, Nick being the exception.

"Bring me a shot too," I said.

It'd be necessary soon. My insides hummed as my body burned through the last of the dosage I'd taken. Nick went without a word, leaving me alone with the slow onset of my craving.

The less morphine remained, the easier it would be for the monster I was to shake it off. As it was, I grew more aware of Ali, peaceful in her bed. I could hear her breathe. The feel of her heartbeat was only barely out of my reach.

I put my knife down and braced my hands on the cool marble counter. Nick was right. What had I been thinking? I didn't want her to be defenseless against the griffs who might catch her trail, but who'd defend her against me? Against the medicated monster I was?

Ali turned in her sleep with a soft sigh of sheets and breath. My grip tightened. I had to keep my control. She'd done nothing to deserve me as her guardian. I was a much bigger danger to her than anything else out there, but yet, I wanted to protect her.

Quiet as a whisper, she keened. It went straight through me. I couldn't stay away. My tread took me straight to her door. I reached up and grasped the handle, holding on tight. Going in would be courting disaster. It would risk us both. But when she whimpered, I opened the door and went in without another thought. Her presence was intoxicating, a gentle touch to a painful scar. I ventured closer, my heart thundering. This was madness. My control was hanging on by the slenderest of tethers, but I couldn't make myself turn away any more than I could tell the sun not to rise.

She'd left the lamp on and it washed her in golden light. Her expression wasn't peaceful. It held so much pain that it gave me pause. I didn't want to hurt her. Didn't want to betray her trust. Her eyes opened and she looked at me. Her gaze was bruised, tired.

"He left," she murmured, dabbing at her eyes. Then she sobbed.

I was by her side before I had time to blink, pulling her into my arms. She curled into me, wrapping her arms around my waist. Her body shook as she silently cried. I rubbed her back, somehow aching for her sake. Aching for her. My true nature wanted to absorb her into me. To draw her vibrancy into my being and feed on it for hundreds of years. But then, the man she'd allowed me to become wanted to make her feel better.

Neither version of me could succeed.

Still, I leaned in and kissed her. I closed my eyes, trying to focus on the physical. The warmth she exuded. How rich her skin smelled. I couldn't name her scent, but it was just right. Like the way she felt in my arms, pressing slightly closer even though our kiss was light. I trailed my finger down the side of her neck, savoring her heartbeat, sensing her life out despite myself.

Ali pulled back and searched my face. Her brows furrowed as fear and confusion filled her clear, blue eyes.

"Go back to sleep," I said. My voice sounded gruff. "You need your rest."

She sighed and rested her forehead against my shoulder. "I don't want to sleep any more. Hurts."

I petted her hair. The last of my control slipped from my grasp. It was too easy. She didn't even fight my presence. Instead, she welcomed it. How could I even think of betraying this trust? More importantly, how would I get out of the door in time?

"Try," I said, trying to convince us both.

Easier said than done. I didn't even want to release her.

"Okay," she said with a sigh, lying back.

Somehow, I managed to let her. I squeezed my eyes shut, trying to force myself to put distance between us. If I didn't... God I didn't even want to imagine. No that wasn't true. Everything in me imagined the ecstasy of consuming the energy keeping her alive.

I had to leave. Now. *Right now.* But then she turned and curled about me.

Her fingertips caressed my hand over the mark she'd given me centuries ago. "Thank you."

"For?"

"For being here whenever I wake up." She yawned. "Makes me feel better…knowing you're here."

I swallowed a lump in my throat. If she only knew what it took out of me. "Sleep well."

I sat there, frozen in place, watching her breaths slow down as she drifted into trusting sleep. Her energy drew me. Called me.

The rustling carpet warned me that Nick was near, but he stabbed me with the syringe before I thought to pull my senses away from Aleria. The needle slamming into my carotid artery hurt like hell.

I grunted and wrapped my hand about Nick's wrist, but he didn't hesitate. In fact, to judge from the intense spurt with which the juice shot into my system, he'd smashed the plunger in with his free hand.

My eyesight went fuzzy. I toppled to the ground as soon as I rose to my feet. Nick had OD'ed. Probably on purpose.

Asshole. Didn't he know I had a morning shift tomorrow?

ALERIA

The sun shone brightly into my room by the time I woke up again. I yawned and stretched, thinking back to last night's kiss. A blush burned my cheeks, but I didn't regret the way I'd acted with Ryan. Not really. No one could regret a kiss that good.

I sat up and took stock of my surroundings. It was quiet. Eerily so. Had Ryan left without waking me? Would I be okay alone?

Berating myself, I brushed my hand back over my hair, combing it a bit with my fingers. Of course I'd be fine. I didn't need Ryan to babysit me all the time. For heaven's sake, one little kiss didn't mean he had to let me know where he was going. I gripped my sheets for a few seconds longer. I could do this. I could face one day alone.

Damn it. It didn't feel right to be so scared all the time.

I got out of bed.

Manhattan stretched out beyond my picture window with what looked like thousands of skyscrapers. Millions of people went about their lives, but no sound of it came into my room.

A flash of movement startled me. I stopped and faced it, then scowled. A mirror. My reflection was a sight. My clothes were wrinkled from sleeping in them and to begin with, they'd never fit right. I resembled a beggar rather than Ryan's guest. Never mind. I didn't hear anyone in the apartment, so no one would know how I looked. I'd take a shower and figure out how to at least iron my clothes. After breakfast.

My stomach rumbled in agreement with my intention to eat. It would be nice to have something other than hospital food. Would I remember how to cook, though? Did I even know how before the crash? I shook my hands in an attempt to get rid of my nerves. Toast. I could handle toast. If I really couldn't remember anything else.

The carpet hugged my bare feet as I walked out of my room. The living area was quiet. The kitchen's tiled floor chilled my toes. Ryan hadn't said anything about helping myself, but he had to expect me to if he wanted me to stay here alone while he went to work. He wouldn't mind if I made myself something to eat.

I opened the fridge and inspected its contents. A surprising variety of food, for a guy. On the other hand, he was a doctor, so maybe he was more focused on maintaining a healthy, balanced diet. Slowly, a sense of how I cooked trickled back into my memories. Lovely. At least I wouldn't be completely useless in the kitchen.

I heard someone pad up behind me and gasped. When I turned, I found Ryan standing there, pale and swaying slightly.

"Are you okay?" I asked, taking in his rumpled appearance. Apparently, he'd also gone to sleep in his clothes. At least I did it because the lost-and-found outfit I wore was the only one I had. What was his reason?

"Mm…fine…" He blinked and squinted as if trying to make his eyes focus. "Just—" His brows drew together and he rubbed his neck. My gaze followed the motion to a bruise on its side.

"What happened?" I went to him for a closer inspection. The bruise was more or less the same color as an eggplant. Close up, I could make out a puncture wound in his skin. "Who did this?"

"Nick," he said. His breath fanned my temple.

"Why?" I asked, taking a step back.

He followed, a lazy smile tugging the corners of his mouth. "You," he said.

My heart fluttered. "Me?"

"Mmm. You. You're…difficult to resist."

The fluttering increased. I cleared my throat and went to the fridge. "Oh?" Oh good. I managed to sound non-idiotic. I glanced his way in time to see his emphatic nod.

"He dosed me to keep you safe. The idiot shot me up with too much morphine. I spent hours waiting for my system to clear."

"Morphine?"

"I use it to keep my—" He ran his fingers over the bite mark I'd given him. "—at bay."

I ducked into the fridge and took out an armful of stuff. Busy was good, very good. It helped me gather the thoughts he'd scattered by being so close. "So you use morphine to stay under control?"

"Yup." I caught sight of him as he started to make coffee.

"How does that work?" I took a look at what I'd taken out. Eggs, ham, two blocks of cheese, peppers, and more tomatoes than I could ever use. Omelets it was, then. I'd still need to put a cartload of tomatoes back.

I did it fast, hoping he didn't notice.

"Morphine diffuses griffons' power, which makes it fade back. With it, our power lust."

The last two words hung heavy in the air, even as a spark of familiarity lit somewhere in the back of my mind. I had no idea why, but I knew this fact in the same way I knew the ingredients to an omelet. Ryan fidgeted with cups and the sugar bowl, clearly uncomfortable with this subject.

"Do you want something to eat?" I asked to change it to something safe. "I'm making omelets."

"Sounds good. Coffee?"

"Please." I stopped when I realized I didn't know how I took it.

Ryan turned on the machine. "What would you like to try? Black? Sugar? We need to figure out what you prefer."

He made it sound so normal I had to smile, feeling a warm flood of gratitude to him. "What do you suggest?"

"Black and bitter. Then you decide if you like sweeter, or with cream or whatever."

"Okay." I went in search of a pan, not really seeing what I was doing.

"Ali," he murmured, moving up behind me. "It'll be fine. I promise." He rested his hands on my shoulders, squeezing gently. "You'll get into a routine. Feel comfortable…"

"What if I never remember?" I whispered. My body felt so frail all of a sudden. Weak. Perhaps it could also betray me the way my mind had.

"You will." His hands continued to work the knots out of my shoulders and back.

How could a girl not relax? I sighed deeply and

nodded. He opened a cupboard I had already searched and pulled out a pan. He handed it over and went to the counter where he started with prep.

We worked side by side in comfortable silence, but as we went on, curiosity got the better of me. I glanced toward the scar on his hand. He was so different from the monster in my dream. Instead of intimidating me, he helped me. Instead of inspiring fear, something about him drew me.

"Can I ask something personal?" I asked, whisking the eggs. The percolator bubbled away, filling the area with a rich, earthy coffee aroma.

"Only if I can ask one in return." He smiled.

What the heck? It wasn't as if I could remember my secrets. I nodded. "What made you become a doctor?"

He carved up some peppers, seemingly devoting all his attention to it. "Someone very smart told me I could be more than what I'd settled to be." He caught my gaze and held it. "I figured helping people would be a good way to make up for the life I'd led up to that point."

Something about his eyes wouldn't let go. A vulnerability. Almost a fear. But of what? Something about him told me I needed to say something.

I raked my teeth over my lip and smiled gently. "I think that's admirable."

The shadows in his eyes went away, and his green eyes shone with something I couldn't define. "Why thank you." He caressed my lower arm as he added the peppers into the pan.

His touch raised goose flesh on my skin. I pretended to concentrate on the frying eggs. He didn't ask his question, so we went on and finished the omelets. I took the plates to the table by the picture window and he brought the cups. We dug in, glancing at each other every now and then.

"What did you dream last night?" he asked. "Who left?"

The food turned stale in my mouth, but fair was fair. "His name's Luc." I frowned a little. "At least, that's what I thought it was. In my dream."

Ryan set down his knife and fork, leaning against his chair's back. "Want to tell me about it?"

"It wasn't a nice dream," I murmured, glancing out the window.

"I know." He put his hand over mine and gave a little squeeze. "Your choice. It might make things easier for you. Talking about them."

I stared at our hands, then turned mine so our palms touched. Things didn't feel as scary with him here. I didn't feel so alone. Not just because someone was with me, but because *Ryan* was with me, holding my hand and watching for the smallest indication of what I wanted.

I met his gaze and nodded. "Okay."

I watched the other debutantes dance, letting the ebbs and tides of waltz music soothe my impatience. This wasn't my first coming out, but it was my first one in Britain, and it would be decades before I looked too old to bother. My family would never fit into British Society if I didn't take part, so I had to put up with the tradition of being ogled by dandies and dukes, wishing to hell I could be out there doing my true duty. I whipped my fan open and swished it about smartly, trying to drain my vexation into the action.

Everything around me glittered. The majestic chandelier above the dance floor, the crystal tumblers for punch, the ladies' jewels. The Empire style had made it into London. Not one of the debutantes wore anything else.

Another of the young men attending asked me to add his name to my dance card, which I did, although not with a song in my heart.

They tried hard, the ones who wanted to marry, but I wouldn't. Not ever. I'd seen how painful it was for my father to wait for my mother's return to his side. I wouldn't be able to stand it. Most of the young lords were mortal, which would be even worse.

They wouldn't come back.

The man went off to get us something to drink, so I let my attention drift back to the dancing couples floating over the glossy wooden floor. Most of the girls wore white, like me. In my case, though, the color was a tad ironic. My face heated at the thought, and I fanned my face to cool myself.

"Now there's a thought I'm dying to hear." Luc Davenport's deep, sonorous voice embraced me. It was the sweetest sound I'd heard in over fifty years.

I cried out softly and threw my arms about his neck. It'd been a lifetime since I'd seen him last, which was always sad, because he was my best friend in the whole world. He laughed softly in my ear as he hugged me.

"Later, you better find a good reason for hugging me like someone you knew for years."

True, but right then, it didn't matter. "Hmm. You're a

family friend."

"Recently returned from France."

That caught my attention. I stepped back. His posture was prouder than before, his brown eyes more serious. He'd brushed back his black hair so much neater than I was used to seeing. Next I noticed his cavalry officer's uniform. It suited him perfectly. The dark blue jacket fitted him as if it had been custom made. Its buttons shone as if polished.

"War?" I frowned, shivering at the thought of losing him for another of his life-times.

He nodded. "I have a short leave, though." He took my hand and led me to my mother, resplendent in her dark green silks.

Her face lit the moment she laid eyes on him. "Luc! How wonderful to see you again. Come to claim my daughter's hand?" Her eyes, so similar to mine, danced.

"If she'll have me," he said, glancing my way. I tried to laugh it off, but I knew that look. It was the conversation I'd been avoiding for three of his lives. He returned his attention to my mother. "May I waltz with your daughter, madam?"

"Of course," my mother said. "Do go greet my husband later, though. He'll want to see you."

He bowed from the hip, then led me to the dance floor. We started dancing, moving together like two people who had danced together for hundreds of years. Which we had. Our hands automatically sought the familiar places on which to rest while we moved, perfectly synchronized to each other, even though it was the first time we partnered for the waltz. For a long time we said nothing, just whirling about the floor to the slow rhythm the orchestra dictated. He caressed the back of my hand with his thumb. It felt as if he burned the pattern into my skin.

"I couldn't stop thinking about you," he murmured, pulling me as close as he dared. I closed my eyes, savoring the warmth of his embrace. It was like coming home after a long absence. No matter when last I'd been in his arms, it felt just like I remembered, protective, loving, and gentle at the same time.

"I missed you," I answered.

Luc led us spinning around the floor, then laughed with exuberance and tugged me outside through the French doors. After the heat and oppressive humidity of the ball, the crisp night air in the garden was like a balm to my soul. I closed my eyes and inhaled, enjoying the slight chill in the air. Luc put his hands to my waist and pulled me to him. I didn't resist. Truth was, I wanted to forget. Just for a while. I wanted to be home and enjoy it.

His kiss was as soft as a butterfly's wings, as if he'd decided to test me first. Succeeding there, he deepened the kiss, demanding more. I gave in to him willingly, moaning softly. It had been years since someone touched me like this. Not since the Russian.

Luc's fingers tangled in my hair and caressed my shoulders, warming me more. His touches were reverent, loving. I cupped his jaw between my hands, kissing him deeply. I wanted so much to give him what he wanted. I wanted to be the woman he'd dreamed me to be.

He moaned softly, drawing me closer, but I pressed my hand against his chest, turning my head away.

"We can't," I whispered.

"Why not?" he asked, trailing touches down the

exposed part of my upper back. "We love each other."

"Where would that leave us tomorrow morning?"

He stiffened. "On the way to Gretna Green."

I sighed and shook my head. It always came down to this. He loved me with a devotion any of the girls dancing inside could only wish for, but he'd never given up on me. Every single time, he died alone. It broke my heart.

"Don't do this again," I said.

He dropped his arms away, then ruined his hair by raking his hand through it. "Damn it, Aleria. I'd do anything for you."

"Then let me go," I begged. "This hurts me as much as it does you."

"Give in, then."

"That would hurt more."

He sighed and leaned in, giving me a tender kiss. "I'll always love you," he said, then went inside, leaving me in the cold. I watched him leave, knowing it'd be another lifetime before I saw him again.

Ryan's brows furrowed, but he said nothing.

"That's all I remember," I said. "Nothing else. Not when we met. Not whether I saw him again—"

"But you know it's real?" He gave my hand another squeeze.

I nodded. "I can't explain, but there was a depth to the dream. As if there's a history to it. I can't remember what, but it's there."

"I understand." He grimaced. "I wish it was a happier dream. Now you need a pick-me-up. After breakfast, I'm taking you shopping."

NICK

I opened my third pack for the day and put a cigarette into my mouth. For about the millionth time, my attention slipped to the clock mounted above Romano's desk. Almost time. I hated the thought of what I might find at Ryan's apartment. What had I been thinking? I should have shot him up twice. Made sure he couldn't even stand.

Shit. I lit the cigarette, frowning at myself. If I'd overdosed him more than I had, Aleria would have been completely defenseless. Before, she would have been able to take care of herself no problem. Now…we just didn't know. Maybe she'd remember her fighting skills, but I couldn't depend on it.

Romano lifted an eyebrow at me. "In a hurry?"

I forced myself to lean back in my chair and smoke. "No, just bored."

"Good. I was hoping for that drink."

Inside, my control strained, on the edge of snapping. I wanted to find her, know where she was, that she was okay. But it would be a stupid thing to do. The Firm killed rogues the moment they found us.

I couldn't call, either. There was no way I could explain to Romano if he figured out that I was in contact with someone who was supposed to be dead. Romano would see my hiding the fact that Ryan had faked the primary witness's death as obstruction of justice. Or maybe not, since she couldn't remember. Except he'd think she could, because why else would we go through so much trouble to hide her?

He couldn't ever know the truth.

"Yo Parker. You still with me, man?"

I frowned, running my fingers over the old *Carnevale* mask I always kept on my desk. "I have a date tonight."

Romano's expression eased up. "She hot?"

In more ways than one. "Yeah." My attention wandered back to the clock.

"What time are you seeing her?"

"I'm meeting her as soon as I leave."

Romano smiled. "Well then, pretty boy, get going. I'll cover for you."

"You sure?"

"Of course I'm sure, partner. I owe you a few favors."

"But the case…"

His smile faded. "It's pretty much one big dead end. No one in the task force is getting anywhere. I'll call you if something develops."

"Thanks, man." I shut down my computer and put my desk into something resembling order.

"Sure. Maybe if this one sticks we can go on a double date. Carla loves them."

"We'll see," I hedged. "Don't hesitate to call."

"I won't."

I dropped my pack of cigarettes into my pocket and grabbed my keys. Outside our office was the usual chaos of the bullpen. Phones rang and people talked, yelled and whispered. I only just reached the lift when my own cell phone rang. I took it out holding my breath. Romano. My breath whooshed out and I returned to our office, where I found him pacing like a madman, eyes bugging at the file gripped in his hands.

"New development?" I asked, and he stopped.

He looked up at me, completely bewildered. "All the witnesses said the two terrorists stood by the cockpit, right? They definitely would have been wounded as badly as Ms. Tyson or worse, right?"

"Right." Save for the fact that Ryan had forged her files. I frowned. Why was Dean questioning common sense?

"Right." He resumed his pacing, flicking his way through the pages. "Then how did they walk away from the crash and hijack a car?"

I reeled as if Romano had clipped my head with a heavy club. "What?"

Romano took out two composite pictures, then turned his computer screen to reveal two photos. They belonged to the two terrorists the task team had identified by process of elimination.

The terrorists had walked away from the crash. My stomach dropped to the floor. Immortals. Given Aleria's fight with them, I wagered they were griffons. Now I wanted to throw up. This would draw everyone's attention. The Firm would know about this by tomorrow. They'd start cleaning up, and I didn't want to be connected to the case when they did. But damn it, I didn't want to quit. I didn't want to lie to Romano, either, but I couldn't explain the truth about our existence. This was a nightmare.

I needed to talk to Ryan, but first, I needed to calm

Romano down. "Weird," I said, frowning. "We can't let this leak out. The press would have a field day."

Romano nodded and went to his computer. "They'd make it into something from a horror movie."

Which it pretty much was. "Exactly."

I waited for him to type the instructions. "Do you have the BOLO out for the car?"

"Yeah."

"Okay. I think I want that drink you offered after all."

Romano ran his hand down his face. "What about your date?"

"She'll just have to understand." I'd have to find a way to call Ryan. "Come on. There's nothing we can do until someone finds the car."

"Right. Right." We headed out. "Nick." He waited for me to look at him. "This isn't possible, is it?"

Those two griffs had to be in pretty bad shape. Even though we were powerful, our regeneration didn't kick in as fast as a phoenix's did. But it was possible.

I stopped, frowning. That was why they picked that particular flight. They had to know Aleria was on it. They wanted to use her to regen and walk off unscathed. And draw the whole human world's attention with it. Oh… fuck.

"Nick?"

I shook myself out of it. "No. No, it isn't." Not if I had any say about it.

NICK

We went to a pub close to the FBI building. I casually slid my hand down my side to check that my gun was in place. It was.

Romano caught me in the act. "You okay?" he asked, glowering towards a dark alley we passed. The man had been paranoid since the day we met. "You look jumpy."

I peered into the alley, then back at him. "You're a fine one to talk. Maybe you rubbed off on me."

He scowled at me, but said nothing. Usually I didn't mind his tendency to be quiet. In fact, I preferred it. Not tonight, though. Tonight, I had too many things to worry about. Like how I'd be able to let the Firm clean up without it noticing I was on the case, because this one would shoot straight up to the boss. For all I knew, the news was already headed his way. He'd recognize his youngest son in seconds.

I rubbed my hand down my face. Served me right for picking some heroic job where clean-ups sometimes needed to happen. No matter which way this went, I'd need to quit and start again. Somewhere far, far away.

I'd have to leave Aleria with Ryan.

No chance in hell.

The pub was a small place located not too far from the local precinct, so its patrons mainly consisted of off-duty cops, and sometimes their girlfriends, wives, or, depending on the guy, both, but never at the same time. It wasn't a fancy place by any means. The benches were wood with leather seats. The lights all had beer logos. The pool table had about eight people around it on quiet nights, but with the owner a former cop and all-round nice guy, the pub was popular. For now, the pub would be quiet, which was exactly what I needed. Once the shifts changed, things would pick right back up.

I went in and sat at the bar, ordering a vodka neat. By the time Romano arrived at my side, I was nursing my second. I missed the days when I could still smoke inside. I could have injected nicotine into my blood stream right now, but first, I needed to sit down and think. I closed my eyes, searching for a way out of this mess that wouldn't fuck up the nice life I'd built, but I couldn't find one.

Even by my fourth drink, I couldn't calm down to figure anything out. This wasn't good. It meant my brain had picked up on something I hadn't. Something supernatural. Something dangerous. And I couldn't figure out what it was.

Then he stood next to me. Six-foot-five, brown hair, buzz cut. Features that seemed to have been carved out of marble. Mean, dark eyes and a sneering smile. Oh, and a bouncer's body. His name was Alick. Fuck, I *really* hadn't wanted to see him again. Ever.

"Well, well," Alick said, his sneer quirking up a bit more. "I heard you were in town. Been looking for you for a while."

My muscles tensed up, but I kept drinking. Alick had to be here to kill me. Unless, of course, I burned through

69

my juice and killed him first. I savored my excellent and expensive vodka, because the odds of dying within the next thirty minutes were about fifty-fifty. "*Finally found me, then?*" I asked, flipping over to Gaelic. Not the sort people talk now. Ryan's Gaelic; the extinct sort he'd taught us back when we were friends. It felt like my old life. It tasted terrible on my tongue.

He snorted and sat down on my other side, ordering a scotch. "*Who's your friend?*" he asked.

"*Partner at work.*"

Romano, bless him, kept drinking, acting as if me speaking anything but English was perfectly normal to him. Typical cop. The moment something strange happened, they perked up, paid attention, and pretended not to.

Alick sipped his scotch. "*I'm looking for Ryan.*"

I closed my eyes and let out a slow breath. How nice, the griffon hunter would have two powerful rogues and a phoenix protector to take home. Thing was, Ryan'd fuck him up in a heartbeat. "*Look, I could tell you, but I doubt you'd want to meet him.*"

Alick rotated the tumbler on the bar mat, frowning. "*Actually, no. I don't. But the boss wants to talk to him.*"

I had to laugh at that. "*Talk. Mhmm. Sure.*"

"*We're calling everyone in. Even you lot.*"

I chuckled, but his expression told me he was serious. And I'd know. Alick, Ryan and me used to run together for centuries. "*Why?*"

"*Juiced up, aren't you?*"

"*Really? Do we need to do this here?*" I tilted my head in Romano's direction, where he was still playing stupid. I sure as hell didn't want him to see anything go down if worst came to worst, or he'd be dead.

"*Why not? Maybe he knows Ryan's whereabouts.*"

I narrowed my eyes, meeting his gaze. "*I didn't know you want to die.*"

He laughed and took a sip. "*Look, there's trouble. Some of the newer guard have grown ambitious and split off. They're for anarchy and ruling the world.*"

"*But we already do—*"

"*Publicly.*"

I scowled and pushed my glass back at the barman. "Make it a triple," I said, briefly going back to English.

"*It'll be war,*" Alick stated with chilling certainty.

What the hell. It wasn't like there was a point to trying to contain the news now. "*I think it's already started. You know the plane crash?*"

"*Don't tell me.*"

"*Two of us. They walked off the site and hijacked a car.*"

Alick blew out a litany of curses, pressing his iced drink to his brow. "*We need Ryan, Niko.*"

Which, of course, gave us another problem. Alick had spent hundreds of years tracking rogues. Eventually, he would track Ryan down, and when he did, he'd find Aleria. Sadly for us, he'd recognize her as well. "*Look. I'll tell him. Give me your number.*"

Alick dug his hand into his breast pocket and flipped a card onto the bar. "*We can't wait long,*" he said and got up, leaving me to pay the bill.

Sonovabitch. The barman made to stop him, but I held up my hand. "I'll pay."

Romano faced me as soon as Alick was out the door, his sharp cop expression back on his face. "Want to explain what that was?"

71

"My past," I said, frowning. Somehow, I still had the feeling we were being watched.

His brows knitted together. "Are you in some sort of trouble?"

A ton of it, but I shook my head. "Nothing for you to worry about." I took a long drink. A pity. Surviving an encounter with Alick should have made the vodka taste better, but his news made it go sour in my stomach.

"You looked like he stepped on your grave."

"It's fine."

"And why does he want Ryan?"

I sighed. "He's a school friend."

"Interesting that you all keep bumping into each other," Romano remarked

"He's arranging a reunion." I downed my drink and stood. "I gotta go."

"To Ryan?" The question was innocent enough, but I knew this was trouble. Romano would eventually demand the truth. I couldn't give it. I'd lose the first and only friend I'd made in a long time.

I patted his shoulder, then picked up the card. I casually ran my fingers over its surface, but if there was a bug in it, I couldn't find it. "Yeah. Alick asked me to get Ryan to call him. See you."

I dropped some bills on the bar and headed to the door, but Romano's voice stopped me.

"If he's a friend from school, why didn't you just take him to Ryan?"

Damn it. "Let's just say they don't get along either."

"Right." He wore an expression I didn't like. One telling me he'd start digging as soon as I left.

I sighed and left anyway.

ALERIA

The mall Ryan and I went to glimmered like polished crystal. Chandeliers hung from high ceilings, adding light to the rays flooding through majestic windows. The place was full of people, rushing this way and that. None of them seemed to notice the beauty around them.

I watched humanity flow about me as we walked, fascinated. The people wore clothes so different from what I'd dreamed of so far. Tighter, shorter, almost overtly masculine, and yet… not. I was dressed differently too, wearing the same jeans and t-shirt Ryan had brought from the lost and found—freshly ironed.

Whatever I'd worn on the day of the crash, my only tangible connection to my life, had been destroyed. Which left me only with fractures and shadows instead of memories.

Ryan's hand slipped into mine, drawing my attention back to him. "You're frowning again," he said gently.

"Sorry," I said. "Just…thinking about the clothes I'd worn. I don't even know what they were."

His expression softened and he gave my hand a squeeze. "Hey. What you wore doesn't matter. Just think. You could have decided on comfort over style. Then your clothes would have told you you're a slob, even if it wasn't actually true."

Ryan was right, but they would have been a tangible connection. Still, I half-smiled. It was sweet of him to try so hard to make me feel better. He beamed at me and drew me closer to his side, curving his arm around my shoulder. The proximity to him sent thrills through me, as did his musky scent. I knew he could be dangerous, but being with him like this, I felt completely safe.

I put my arm around his waist and gave him a little hug, letting my gaze wander from place to place as we walked. The mall was filled with amazing displays, but one stood out so much, it brought me to a complete stop.

Mannequins dressed in party clothes, all wearing Carnival masks. Ryan jolted me a little before stopping before the marvelous display of designer dresses and drama.

"What is it?" he asked. "See something you like?"

"No, I… The masks." I pointed at one and moved away from him, toward the display.

"Well hello there, beautiful." Luc's lovely voice caressed the back of my neck and I squealed, giving him the biggest hug I could.

"You followed us here?" I asked, holding on to him as if he might disappear at any moment. When we'd left France, I'd left Luc behind and with him, my heart. Oh how I'd cried that day. He'd looked my age back then.

I stepped back and looked up at his face. Now he was somewhere in his twenties. He now looked older than me, while I barely seemed old enough to go to my first *Carnevale* party. The realization sent a stab through me and I lowered my gaze.

He was a man now, and I...I didn't even know what I was. A woman trapped in a child's body? A freak of nature. Either way, it wouldn't do to seem overly familiar with someone in public. It wasn't proper. Venice might have been home to Casanova, but in reality, life here was strict. I sent a furtive glance to my companion, who at least was kind enough to stay at a discrete distance for the duration of this conversation.

"We're both here," Luc said. "Armand tired of France."

I scowled up at him despite myself. "Please tell me he's not going to the Doge's party."

He frowned at me. "What if he is?"

"He'll spoil it," I lamented, causing Luc's frown to deepen. He always was devoted to his twin.

"I do wish you two would get along." Luc said.

"And I do so wish he'd stop being an ass." Or that he'd stop breathing, for that matter. I turned back to the display of *Carnevale* masks. I still needed to find a mask to match the dress I planned to wear to the party.

I heard Luc's heavy sigh behind me. "At least you're still glad to see me," he said and joined me by the window. "I missed you."

"I–I..." I wanted to say I missed him too, but if I had never before realized what a difference our lifespans made, I felt it keenly now. He'd be reborn long before I was, and then he'd outgrow me again and again. When I had my rebirth, it could take centuries for us to be together again.

It wasn't a way for us to live.

I swallowed my words and went to the next window, dashing at my tears. I tried to hide it, but Luc was too perceptive.

He caught my arm and forced me to face him. "Don't," he murmured, pulling me closer to him. "I'm here now."

I sobbed and held onto him. He stroked my back and whispered loving words into my ear. I felt the strength in his body, the play of his muscles beneath my fingers. But no matter how close we were, we'd never be together.

My heart ached as if that moment with Luc had just happened, instead of occurring hundreds of years ago in Renaissance Italy.

Ryan moved up behind me and wrapped me in his arms. We met each other's eyes in the window's reflection.

"Did you remember something?"

"Another thing with Luc." I didn't want to talk about it yet. It hurt too much. "Let's go."

He nodded and took me to another shop, where he insisted I try on everything my heart desired.

* * *

Ryan took my hand as we rode the taxi home, sitting close between bags overflowing with "necessities" he'd bought me. I liked the feel of his touch. Soft and gentle, but strong for all that. I smiled, avoiding his eyes by keeping my attention on the faint scar on his hand. I lightly traced my finger over the crescent.

"Thank you," I said, finally gathering the nerve I

needed to meet his gaze. "I had a wonderful time."

His beautiful mouth quirked up, and his eyes shone. "So did I. I've never laughed so much in my life."

"Oh, I doubt that," I said. "Old creature you are."

He chuckled. "Yeah, well. My years on earth haven't really been a comedy." He sobered, pulling back, but I didn't want him to. Before I really thought about it, I reached my free hand up to his chin, turning toward him more. He stiffened, but closed his eyes with a soft sigh as if soaking in the feel of my touch.

Ryan tilted his head and peeked at me through his long, dark lashes. "Nothing to be sympathetic about," he said. "You've had a challenging life too."

Not like I knew anything about that. I offered him a vague shrug, trying to ignore the twinge in my heart. "Tell me more about yours."

"Not much to tell. My dad expected me to keep doing work I no longer liked. My life grew empty until I met that girl I mentioned. She taught me I was more than what I thought I was, so I left and never looked back."

I would have asked more questions, but he turned his head and kissed the inside of my wrist as if he'd done it a million times before.

A tiny but intense thrill shot through me. My breath hitched and he lifted an inquiring eyebrow. I caressed my fingers over his jaw, coarse from afternoon stubble. We met each other's gaze, trapped each other. His eyes darkened to the gray-green of a stormy sea and, for a breathless moment, I thought he wanted to kiss me. I wanted him to.

The taxi came to a halt, breaking the spell. I glanced out to see we had arrived at Ryan's place.

Ryan released my hand and got out. He summoned the porter while I collected some of my shopping bags. I did my best to deal with my disappointment. Try as I might to rationalize away the moment we'd had, I knew it was there. I also knew it was as significant to Ryan as it was to me. He ducked in and paid the cabbie, keeping his gaze averted. What was he hiding? I frowned and got out after him.

Ryan, the porter, and I trooped into the building, lugging the shopping with us.

"There's an FBI agent waiting to see you, sir," the porter said.

Ryan tensed. "Agent Parker?"

"Yes, sir."

"I expected him to return," he said, but the hard edge to his voice belied his words. "You can bring up the bags later."

"Very good, sir."

Ryan dropped his bags right there and went to the lift, leaving me standing in the lobby. After all the little touches and laughter, this felt like an ice cube to the back of my neck. Was he angry at me because Nick was here? No, that would be stupid. This had to be about the old rivalry going on between them. The one they thought I didn't notice.

I set down my bags and followed Ryan, arriving just as the lift opened. We got in and he punched his finger into the top floor's button. He looked over at me when the doors closed.

"Have you remembered him?"

His coldness stung. Maybe it *was* me he was angry at. I edged away from him. Standing close to him didn't feel right anymore. "Nick?"

"Yeah."

I shook my head, but Nick's absence in my memories wasn't for lack of trying to remember what he meant to me. I'd attempted to place him ever since we met at the hospital, but all I got back were little bits and pieces. Still, something about the hardness in Ryan's expression told me to keep this to myself. "Why?"

"Because he won't back off," he said, crossing his arms. His biceps bulged and tensed.

I frowned, focusing on his eyes again. "Why do you want him to? Is he dangerous?"

"Not like me," he muttered, leaning back. "Seemingly not to you." His voice sounded brittle. Aching. He was hurting. Badly.

"Ryan, is this okay? Me living here?"

"It's fine."

And yet, everything about him said it wasn't. I reached for him, yearning to make things better, but the lift pinged and the door opened on our floor. Before I could make contact, Nick's footsteps thundered towards us.

"Why didn't you answer my calls?" he demanded, shoving at Ryan's chest.

Ryan tensed, clenching his jaw, then punched Nick with enough force to send him sprawling. I gasped and dropped to my knees by Nick's side.

"Fuck…" Nick groaned and sat up, blinking at me. "That was a bad idea. He needs to calm down."

I glimpsed a movement by the apartment's door. Ryan unlocked it and went in. He slammed it shut. Something about Ryan was different. Dangerous. My heart thundered and I swallowed back a huge lump of fear. "I-

I'll go talk—"

"No," Nick barked, pinching his nose to staunch the blood flowing from it. "Stay here."

"And what? Let you upset him more?"

Nick leaned his head back and I shot away before he had a chance to answer. I went into the suite and locked him out. As soon as I stepped away from the door, I knew I was out of my depth. My heart thundered so hard it hurt. My breaths came in short bursts. Something inside me buzzed with knowledge that someone of immense power stood nearby.

One glance about the living room said he wasn't there.

"Ryan?" My voice sounded unnaturally loud.

"Ali. Get out."

His voice came from his bedroom. It sounded drawn tight, gritted out through teeth grinding in pain. I ignored every single instinct and rushed to him instead.

He groaned the moment I entered the room, even though he had his back toward me. A still-full syringe dropped out from between his fingers. He turned to face me, but it wasn't the Ryan I knew. This was the one I remembered from my nightmares. I cried out and went for the door, but he had his arm constricting about my neck before I took a step. I tried to scream, but the sound couldn't get past my throat.

He kicked the door shut and dragged me away from it. *No!* I rammed my foot into his and followed that with a solid hit to his abdomen. My instincts kicked in out of thin air. Fire. *Fire.*

I had to get fire. I needed it or I'd die. My thoughts immediately went to the kitchen, but Ryan only grunted and squeezed harder, dimming my view of the door.

Something about him invaded me, filling me with cold dread. Then came a familiar sensation as his soul linked to mine, drawing it out to him. He was going to steal my life. Pull it into himself as easily as he breathed. I sobbed and scratched at his arm, but the draw of his power was too great. He'd consume me in seconds and I had nothing in me to fight it. I whimpered, closing my eyes, trying to reach for fire with my mind, but it didn't work. I had to fight the draw first.

Without warning, his draw stopped pulling. Not letting go, but not killing me either. And then I felt it. A glimmer. The soft warmth of a tiny flame in the distance. That was fine; it was the start I needed to nurture into an inferno. I reached out, focusing on calling the fire to me.

"That's right," Ryan growled. "Kill me. Please..." His voice broke, giving me pause. "Do it!" he shouted, jerking his arm tighter about my throat when I didn't respond.

Try as I might, I couldn't force myself to summon the fire. Tears running down my face, I stroked my hand over his lower arm, waiting for him to consume me.

The pull returned, drawing at my soul once more, but he released a tortured scream and it stopped again. Slowly, his hold on me slacked enough for me to escape, but I stayed rooted where I was. I knew instinctively I was being a fool, but everything I knew about Ryan warred with this. I turned to him and burrowed into his arms, wrapping my own about his waist.

His body tensed and he drew a sharp breath. Finally, I felt another change. The draw was still there, but it was different. I recognized this. While he was no less dangerous, he had stopped being a threat. His hands cupped my face and turned it up. I followed his guidance, watching his face as he lowered his mouth. The contact of our lips was electric. It was life-changing. I wanted more. Groaning, Ryan slanted his mouth over mine, consuming me in a different way. It was a harsh kiss, demanding everything I could give, possessing me whether I wanted to fight it or not.

I wouldn't have wanted it any other way. I moaned, returning the kiss, pulling myself closer to him. This still wasn't the doctor I'd met after the crash, but it wasn't purely the monster either. He slid his hands down my neck, along my shoulders and arms. He grasped the back of my shirt, fusing our mouths and bodies together. His soul drew mine again, but only enough to entwine them as we kissed. The power I felt was intoxicating. Addictive. I wanted more, I wanted everything. If he'd asked for my soul right then, I wouldn't have even thought of declining.

A nearby door slammed open and Ryan released me as if I'd given him a shock.

"Fuck," he rasped, running his shaking hands through his black curls.

I blinked, trying to get enough of me back to respond, but Nick burst into the room seconds later. His face was deformed, eyes blazing at Ryan. Somehow, I recognized the feeling of his power. He was furious.

I gasped and jumped into his field of vision. "I'm okay!" I shouted and pressed my hands against his chest, trying to put some distance between him and Ryan.

Nick tensed, then released a heavy, relieved sigh. "*When you didn't use the flame*—" he spoke Russian, stirring a memory, but not enough to break it loose.

"Wh-what?"

"My lighter." I let him steer me into the living room.

I shut the door. "Oh. Yeah, that's right. I use fire." I blushed.

"Couldn't get in at first. The door was griffon-proof." He released a little laugh and pulled me into his arms. "You scared the shit out of me, Poison."

That one word, "Poison," sent a flash of light through my brain, so bright I moaned and practically collapsed into Nick.

ALERIA

"Alya?" Nick asked, guiding me to a chair.

I drooped down, gripping his arms for stability. "I know you. Knew… Long ago."

"Yes," he said. "What did you remember?"

I met his gaze. His eyes were so blue. "London. A ball."

A sad smile played on his lips. "You were a debutante."

Another year, another ball. Another dress too, ironically white to match Society's expectations of me as a young, eligible, and single woman. I hid amongst a giggling bunch of vapid debutantes, hoping to avoid attention. Despite being courted out of my mind last time, I'd managed to stay firm, but not nearly enough to deter the most determined of my beaus. No. I was simply seen as more challenging. By extension: something the spoilt boys *had* to have.

I blew out a sigh and opened my ostrich feather fan in an attempt to hide my identity a little longer. No one looked my way. At least the vast ballroom filled with partygoers helped to obscure my location, but it was so damnably bright in here that it would only be a matter of time before someone spotted me. Still, I relaxed slightly. It wouldn't do to slip out just yet. Only ninnies with trysts did that.

Instead I settled in for the wait, either for a chance to escape, or to be caught up in the dancing. I let my thoughts wander while I idly waved the fan. Where was Luc now? After that night, he'd vanished again and still hadn't returned. I'd assumed I'd hear of him making a name for himself as a soldier, but nothing reached my ears.

I slapped the fan closed with a hiss of annoyance. Luc had a choice and a life of his own. I had no business worrying about him. Not after I'd made clear that there wasn't a future for us together. I focused on the gossip flowing about me, trying to pretend I shared their short and often silly little lives.

"Well, he'll just have to accept he's not the most attractive prospect this year," one girl said and giggled. "I much prefer the adventure of a Russian prince."

My stomach took a steep dive and I fanned myself again, this time to pretend my creeping blush was from the ballroom's stuffy heat as opposed to the memory of leaving one Russian prince naked and shackled to his bedpost so he couldn't follow my escape to a new life. No, it couldn't be him. He'd be in so much trouble if his friends found out. So would I, if my father knew.

Another pretty girl winked at me. "Try not to catch his eye," she said. "Let us plain ones have some hope?"

I laughed, but it felt strained. People always thought my looks drew them. It wasn't. It was the warmth coming from my soul that attracted people and made them feel safe. Even if they technically should have wanted to kill me. Like the prince I'd shackled. Could this be the same one? I wanted to say no again, but I couldn't. He did promise he'd find me.

I wanted to see if I could sense him out, but truth was, I didn't want to know if it was him. Instead, I gathered my courage and asked. "I've been out of town for a few weeks. What's this wonderful prince's name?"

"Prince Nikolai Yurevich Tyrov."

Oh no. I lowered the fan, then shut it as daintily as I could. "Oh."

He found me. And I needed to be gone before he entered the hall. I pasted a smile on my face. "Excuse me."

I left without hearing their replies, heading straight for the French doors. Sod Society's rules, now wasn't the time for me to be proper. The house belonged to close friends of my family, so I knew this was the fastest way to escape. Out the doors, down the garden, over the wall. A short walk home for supplies and then a trip to Scotland, from where I'd find a ship to anywhere else.

I sensed him behind me before I heard him.

"*Poison,*" he drawled in Russian. "*You were harder to find than I thought.*"

Heat shot to my face and I walked faster, counting on him not making a scene. He laughed and fell in with me, taking my hand onto his arm like a blasted beau. I glared at him, taking in his fashionable but dark clothes, his cued blond hair, his bright blue eyes. Then there was his strong jaw, shaven and cleaner than the last time I saw him, and his muscled body. Everything about him screamed *Rake!* Which he was. I knew that too well from delicious experience. A deep blush replaced the glower, even if I was infuriated at myself.

My drinking in his looks made him appear welcome at my arm. Now I was stuck, unable to draw attention. I glanced towards my father, mercifully still talking to some friends. All of them protectors, and all of them would kill Nikolai on sight.

He patted my hand. "*They won't feel me,*" he promised. "*Thankfully, someone had the vision to make opium dens popular. So right now, my powers are disguised.*"

Well that explained it. I stuck to English, since I couldn't explain knowing Russian to people who might hear me. "So you're—"

"*Not on enough juice for you to trick me again.*"

I winced, drawing a rich chuckle from him. The sound thrilled me despite myself.

"*I find your scheming quite charming,*" he said, his eyes dancing. "*Or I did. That blanket you threw over me was pretty thin for the Russian winter.*"

My ears burned and I ducked my head. "There was a fire burning," I whispered

"Mmm…" he murmured, much closer to my ear than was proper. "*But I'd told my servants not to disturb us.*"

Oh. My stomach fluttered at the hedonistic two days I'd spent in his arms. "S-Sorry?"

He laughed. "*Oh no. Sorry doesn't quite cut it for me. You made me look a fool. Do you have any idea how long it took me to live down being tricked by a mortal?*"

Admitting I was a phoenix, a protector no less, would have been a lot worse for him. I walked a bit faster, straight across the porch and down the steps into the darkened garden. As soon as we were out of sight, I punched him so hard he probably plowed a furrow through the yard with his head. I didn't stay to watch. Instead, I tucked tail and sprinted for the back wall and my escape. I was mere yards from the wall when his weight crashed into my back.

I started to scream, but his hand slapped over my mouth and stifled my screams as he lifted us into the sky.

Nick sat back, watching me. His eyes shone when he met my gaze, as if he relished the thoughts on his mind. It was like a punch to my stomach, almost reminding me of every time we'd locked eyes before. From the intensity of feelings rushing through me, that had happened a great many times, and often. But something about his expression was off. It was guarded.

He sighed and rubbed his jaw. "Will you go check on Ryan? I need to talk to him."

I nodded and stood. "It's urgent, isn't it?"

"Yes." He looked lost, now his anger had faded. Part of me wanted to reach out and tuck back a flyaway shock of blond hair that had come loose above his brow.

I curled my hand into a fist and stood. It wouldn't be right. Not after the kiss I'd shared with Ryan. I walked to the door and heard Nick let out a weary sigh behind me. I knocked, then ventured in. Ryan glanced my way over his shoulder.

"Didn't think he'd let you near me until I'm down."

"Down?"

He lifted the syringe, revealing it was filled to capacity. "Out. Completely and utterly unable to move."

Chewing my lip, I took a few steps closer. "Guess he

figured you would have killed me by now if you wanted to."

"I don't know how I didn't." His hand dropped to his side. "My every instinct is to become that…thing again." He laughed bitterly. "I can't even bring myself to deliver the injection. I don't know how, but I'm managing not to give in to my craving."

I took the syringe from him, gently caressing his hand as I did so. "Maybe you're more than the monster you think you are." He let me roll up his sleeve, revealing quite a few marks and bruises on the inside of his elbow.

He let go of a pained gasp when I pressed the needle through his skin. "Maybe. About earlier…"

Oh, right. It sounded like an apology. I focused on injecting about half the syringe. Hopefully that would do the trick without being too much. "Don't worry. We just got lost in the moment." I drew out the needle and set the syringe aside. "I didn't think anything wrong of it, okay?"

I glanced his way in time to see a smile light up his face.

"Good," he said, taking my hand and drawing me closer. "Because I want to kiss you again."

My heart immediately went back to racing. Just the memory was enough to make me crave his lips. But Nick was outside, and suddenly, kissing Ryan didn't feel quite right either.

"Nick," I murmured, wishing Ryan would ignore me and make me forget my conscience.

He sighed and dropped his hands away. "Right. Let's go talk to the idiot."

RYAN

I frowned as I watched Ali slip out to join Nick once more. Her off-hand comment was like a stab to my heart, so similar was it to the day before I'd left the Firm. *You're more than a mindless killer.* I'd wanted to kill her for her life force. She knew that, but she still looked up at me with those big, blue eyes and told me the complete opposite.

She'd spoken with complete certainty back then. As if she'd known a truth that was hidden from me. Then she spared me when she could have destroyed me, and I had spent the past seventy or so years since trying to make it up to her.

Somehow, my attempts had made her truth my own. It became part of me. It made me become a doctor. Now, it made me able to stop myself from killing her. Or maybe not. Not knowing terrified me. But damn, that kiss blew my mind. It was like sharing in her power without taking it. Amazing on so many levels.

I followed her out and found Nick reclined on my sofa, feet crossed on the coffee table. His expression wasn't the usual show of his not giving a damn. In fact, the concern etched into his face chilled me.

"What?" I demanded. If this was him fussing about Ali, I'd kick his ass.

Call me old-fashioned, but I didn't appreciate the competition he represented. Or the idea that he might have kissed her first. Maybe they'd even had a relationship at some point. I took a deep breath, trying to stay calm. My snapping before wasn't safe.

"We're in deep shit," Nick said. "Especially now that both of us went through our juice."

"Yeah," I said. "They'll hunt now. We'll have to move."

"You won't have time," Nick said. "Alick's already here, looking for you."

I closed my eyes and rocked back on my heels. Shit. Although I hadn't used anywhere near my full power, it had been enough for him to feel it and know it was me. He could be on his way as we spoke. "Wait. How are you still here?"

"The Firm's in trouble," Nick said, and went on to tell me everything he knew.

Oh perfect. My day would continue to improve. I'd basically given away my position, and Alick would track me down. He'd find Ali, and then I'd either have to kill him or he'd kill her. Not much of a contest for me, although if I killed my father's new second in command, I might as well face the fact that I'd die. I rubbed the back of my neck, scowling. My gaze automatically went to Ali who was perched carefully on the edge of her seat, silent, watchful, and trusting. I couldn't let him find her.

"Ali. Stay here. Nick and I need to go."

Her lips parted briefly, then she shot up and shook her head. "No. You don't want to go back."

I drew her to me, holding on tight. Her point was excellent. I'd have to join the fight or die. I'd have to let the monster loose. I didn't want to. Not after the moment I'd just shared with her. But there was hope now. I suddenly had way too much to lose either way. Holding Ali gave me a strength I didn't know I had. She'd formed my life in a few simple words, and now protecting her was my purpose.

No matter what the cost.

Whether I wanted to go or not wasn't relevant. I had to keep Ali safe.

"I'll find a way out of this," I said and placed a tender kiss on the top of her head. "You'll be safe in here, okay?"

She gave me a squeeze and looked up. "Let me go with you. I'll stay out of sight. No one will know I'm there."

I shook my head, tucking a strand of hair behind her ear. "You mean too much to me, Ali. I can't put you at risk."

"I'm not made of glass," she countered, setting her jaw. "I could have killed you before."

"Speaking of which," Nick cleared his throat, drawing our attention. "I'll feel a lot better if you take this." He tossed a lighter our way and Ali plucked it out of the air with graceful ease.

He shot a dark stare at me. Clearly, he thought I was encroaching on his territory. Too bad. If he didn't talk about it, he couldn't stake a claim.

"Won't you need it?" she asked, immediately opening the cap and sparking a flame.

The simple action made my inner monster recoil, but it made me feel a lot better knowing she had it for protection.

"Probably not," I answered for him, and she focused on me again. Which made me feel a lot better too. "Don't open the door for anyone. No matter what they say."

Her mouth turned down. "Fine," she said, then softened a little. "Be careful." Aleria backed out of my hold and went to Nick, giving him a hug too.

His expression instantly eased. "What's this for?" he asked, back to his familiar, cocky attitude. "I'll expect another when I'm back."

She laughed. "Deal."

She gave us both worried looks, then went off to her room as if she couldn't stand to watch us leave.

Nick's gaze followed her, his posture slumping.

"You loved her," I said.

He flicked his attention back to me, his look sharp enough to kill. "Still do. Always will."

I stiffened at the very obvious line he'd drawn. If he thought he'd intimidate me into backing down when it came to Ali, he was gravely mistaken. I smiled without humor and cocked my head at a small angle. Just like old times, which *thrilled* my inner monster for reasons I didn't even want to think about. "Shall we?"

"Sure."

We went to my room, to the walk-in safe with my birthday combination. I opened it and handed him some guns, syringes, and knives before strapping the same to my body under my jacket. So Alick had said they weren't going to kill me, but that didn't mean it was true, and it definitely didn't mean I'd go down without a fight. Story of my life. I'd been battling for so long that even when I went rogue, I continued to stockpile weapons that could do permanent damage to a griffon. Maybe my inner monster had used the collection as his creative outlet because it was all I'd let him do.

I shut the safe and activated the lock. It boomed shut like an iron coffin on the life I'd built over the past few decades. No. It wasn't the end. It *couldn't* be the end.

"You ready for this?" Nick asked, leading the way out.

I glanced at Ali's closed door as we passed it. *Was* I ready for any of this? But my old instincts kicked in. Feelings and fears had to be concealed. Weaknesses eradicated. I straightened my posture and nodded.

The front door swung open when I tried to shut it. I scowled at Nick. He'd destroyed the lock when he thought Ali was in danger. I'd have to replace it before it worked again. Nick glowered right back. Neither of us said anything. We were both at fault.

"We need to break out," I stated instead. "No use hiding the apartment. They already sensed us earlier." We had to draw any risks away from here.

I exhaled and closed my eyes, mentally thanking Ali for being light on the dosage she's given me. It made it just that much easier to find my power and access it.

My true form stirred, already straining at its tether. I sighed and cut it loose, letting my inner monster burn through the morphine as if it was hardly there.

The force of its release was enough to make the apartment's circuitry fizzle. The rush I felt was like nothing else. The city's life force pressed against my awareness. As individuals, mortals' lives were mostly too small to pick up. But together, it felt like the ebbs and flows of an ocean.

My senses grew keener, flooding me with noise, light, sensations and smells. It took me a moment to adjust, to focus only on what was important and let everything else fade to the back of my mind. If I wanted, my ears could pick up conversations from miles away. My eyes could see things too small or too fast for mortals to notice. My skin could feel the air around me. Down to the tiniest change. My sense of smell beat a bloodhound's. I had the strength to punch through bricks. I could fly. I had the speed to almost be invisible to the people around me. But all this sensory input could handicap me if I didn't control what I focused on.

Mmm…it felt good to be back. When I opened my eyes again, I found Nick watching me. I felt his awe, his trepidation, and his short battle to shake free of the morphine's effect.

We left the mortal way, conserving our energy as much as possible. When we fought and used too much power, we *really* started craving to the point where there wasn't any control left. That wouldn't be safe for Ali either, and we would need to stay away until we recovered.

"You know," Nick said, hitting the button to the ground floor. "Every player and his mother is going to come to New York now."

I shrugged. "Good. Saves me the travel expenses to clean up."

Nick chuckled. "True." His smile faded away. "For what it's worth, I'll help."

"Really?" I stared at him, searching for a clue that he wasn't serious. Nick had left the Firm more than a century ago, burning every single one of his bridges behind him. I never thought he'd even consider doing the Firm a service beyond delivering its message to me. "I thought you were done."

"So did I, but those idiots rebelling against the Firm

are dangerous. We need to shut it down or the mortals will find out about us, and we'll have an even bigger mess."

True. Mortals didn't grasp the punishment it was to be immortal. They wanted it, and if I could have, I would have gladly handed it over. But humans could only gain a form of immortality by drinking our blood. The few who had succeeded at sedating us for long enough to get a sip had turned into abominations. Monstrosities. Arch Vampires. They'd been inflicting their brand of immortality on innocent bystanders ever since.

Our first job wasn't to kill each other and other creatures. It was to protect, help, and guide humans.

Somehow, the Firm had managed to do that, despite quite a few fuck-ups on our part. Like our life force addiction. If the rebels revealed our existence, our ability to do our main duty would be destroyed. I felt the same way as Nick, even if most of my motivation was to protect Ali.

"Thanks," I said, glancing his way. So many things went unsaid. Stuff we'd said and done to each other all those years ago. It had ruined our relationship beyond repair. But still, it felt good to know Nick had my back again. Hopefully he felt the same way about me.

We walked about three blocks down when we got our first sense of something approaching. Not a griffon; we would have felt it. Not a phoenix. Not a protector, since we couldn't sense them at all if they were in stealth mode. I frowned and took a breath, inhaling the faint scent of death usually hanging about a vampire.

He came out of an alley, safe enough in the skyscrapers' shade. Strangely enough, he was much less twitchy than I was used to seeing in vampires. He was well-dressed in a black coat and scarf. His straight black hair was styled. There was no sign of a vampire's greed and hunger in his face, which would have made him look quite pleasant if not for the fury burning in his glare.

"What's up with him?" I asked, and Nick glanced over.

The vamp narrowed his eyes, stalked straight over to Nick, and punched him. Nick went down with a grunt. I grabbed the vamp, trying to figure out what was wrong with him. Most of the time, vamps stayed the hell away from us. We killed their clan heads on sight. So for one to walk up and deck Nick was weird as…a griffon kissing a protector rather than killing her.

"You asshole!" the vamp shouted, straining against my grasp. "I've been protecting him for years and you set a pack of griffs on his trail!"

Nick stayed on the ground, gaping up at the vamp. "What are you talking about?"

"Romano!" the vamp shouted, kicking at him.

Nick managed to dodge, but his eyes widened.

"Romano?" I pulled the vamp a bit further away from Nick. "What the hell would griffs want to do with him?"

"Alick's being an asshole," Nick grumbled, rubbing his jaw. "Probably checking to see if I told him anything."

"Did you?" the vamp demanded.

"Do I look stupid?"

The vamp snarled and I wrenched him farther away. "The world is going to hell in a hand basket," I muttered.

"What do you have to do with Romano?" Nick jumped back onto his feet and dusted himself off.

The vamp went limp. "None of your damned

business. But your little friend Alick sent griffs after him to try and find the mysterious and powerful Ryan, and I don't fucking like that."

"Neither do I." Nick squinted at him, then recognition came. "You're Vincent Minnelli."

"Right."

"From where?" I asked.

"New York City."

"What turned you?" I released him.

He didn't go for Nick again. Instead, he smirked at me. "9/11. I was a cop. Got trapped in one of the collapses."

Trust the vamps to dig through the wreckage for easy prey.

Nick's face contorted in pure disgust. "Vince used to be Romano's partner before he got killed and Romano left the NYPD."

"Right. Boy went on the path of vengeance. I made sure to keep him out of trouble."

"Why?" I pressed.

"What the hell else am I supposed to do? My job was to serve and protect."

"But...you're a vamp."

He sent me a nasty glare. "And you're a fucking menace to society, but you don't hear me throwing that around lightly, do you?"

Nick chuckled. "I like him."

"Of course you do." I answered. "He's as much of a wise-ass as you. Look. No worries about Romano, okay? I'm drawing the griffs to me, so they'll leave him alone now. See, I'm the great and mysterious Ryan everyone's looking for."

In the meantime, there wasn't enough distance between me and the apartment. I went on walking. Nick caught up a few seconds later, followed by the vamp. I frowned at Vincent. "You better clear out. We don't know what sort we'll be attracting."

"I can help with the baby griffs."

"You're a baby vamp."

"With razor reflexes, a hair trigger gun, and a killer aim."

"True," Nick said. "Romano always said Vince was the best shot he knew."

"But it's day," I pointed out. "He'll be blinded."

Vince rolled his eyes. "When was the last time you met a vamp? We have polarized sunglasses now." He slipped them out of his pocket and slid them on. Then he walked straight into the sunlight.

NICK

Ryan shook his head and followed the vamp into the light.

I had to smile. "I bet if I'd told you you'd be harboring who you are, and having a vamp for back-up, you'd have laughed and told me to stop drinking."

"Probably," Ryan said, shrugging.

Vince gave us a mock salute, then went off at speed.

"Is he really that good of a shot?" Ryan asked.

I shrugged. "He used to be. He did a tour of duty as a sniper before joining the police. Who knows if he still has the focus."

"Great," Ryan said. "So he might kill us instead."

"Maybe no one'll get killed," I said.

"If we're lucky."

I let that hang in the air and focused on sensing past the huge ball of power next to me. Someone was definitely moving in. A griff. A big player.

"Alick's coming," Ryan said. His range was much wider than mine. A little bonus for being a couple of hundred years older than me.

Alick slowed down just out of sight, then walked up to meet us. "Well, well," he said. "Here you are." He inspected Ryan from top to toe. "Found a phoenix lately? You look like the day you'd left."

Ryan just stared back. "What does the Firm want from me?"

"Your father wants you back in the fold, Ryan. Both of you." Alick's gaze slid away, briefly resting on me. "The Firm's weakened from the inside. We need strong hands to put it back on its course."

"And to wipe out the traitors to our secret," I said. Might as well call a spade a spade. We'd be hunting our own, and it wouldn't be pretty.

Alick glanced my way. "He's offering amnesty to everyone who returns. Even you."

I smiled, but it tasted sour. "Good God, you are desperate."

I had been the first big player to go rogue in ages. My leaving had set me up as their greatest target for centuries. Presumably until Ryan had followed my example.

Alick scowled. "Don't push my buttons, Niko. I haven't the patience for it."

"Nick," I shot back. "I stopped being Russian in the 1800s."

"Not to mention a griffon."

"We both have," Ryan interjected, surprising us both. "So you might want to watch what you say, Alick."

His words made Alick stiffen. "Look. If I had my way, I'd take you out first."

"Too bad you'd die in the attempt." Ryan's lip curled. "Tell my father I'll clean up his mess, but you lot stay away from me. I'm not interested in your piece of shit politics." He turned on his heel and marched away.

Ryan had just publicly turned down his chance at not being hunted. That took guts. Alick glowered my way, but I only shrugged. "Should have watched the attitude."

He narrowed his eyes then shot forward like a flash, aiming straight for Ryan. Before I even had a chance to go after him, something caught my eye. A bullet, buzzing slightly as it flew past me. It slammed into Alick's thigh, plowing him into the sidewalk. He cursed profusely and sat up, inspecting the damage. Blood gushed from the wound.

"Want me to finish the job?" Vince shouted from somewhere nearby. A green dot appeared between Alick's eyes.

I glanced to Ryan. It'd be a lot safer to say yes, but there was something deeply repulsive about killing another griffon. There'd be enough of that soon enough anyway.

A very old hatred deformed Alick's face. "Do it," he spat. "Because if you don't, it'll be my pleasure to get permission to hunt you down like a bird."

The derogatory term for phoenix immediately heated my temper. "If you try, we'll send you home in pieces."

Ryan nodded. "Go on. Get your permission. I'll be waiting. In the meantime, I'll do the real job and fix your fuck-up."

Another bullet flew past, missing Alick's head by an inch. Alick flinched at the dust flying into his face.

"Sorry!" Vince called out. "Finger slipped. Lots of gun, you know? But if you come near anyone under my watch, my finger will slip again. Next time, I won't miss."

We left Alick lying there bleeding, walking further away from the apartment just to put a bit more distance between us and Aleria for now. Hopefully Ryan's power would be enough to keep everyone's attention without them thinking about where it flared up the first time.

After a few miles, Ryan looked at me. "I think we made a mistake, promising to stay and fix the problem while pissing off the Firm."

"Alick shouldn't have been a dick," I said

Vince dropped in by Ryan's other side, casually slinging his gun bag over his shoulder. "So, what now?"

I had to be honest with Vince, especially since he had been watching out for Romano for years. "You do realize they'll hunt you down with us from now on?"

"Yep."

Okay then.

"You've got good control for a vamp," Ryan said. "Especially a young one."

"Habit," Vince said. "I try not to hunt. I get my blood from the black market. Easier to live a normal-ish life when I'm not scenting blood all the time."

Ryan's brows knitted together. "You have a supplier? Reliable?"

"Not really. So I have a few, but they don't really always deliver. Fortunately, the city is full of scumbags."

"But you still avoid hunting?"

He shrugged. "I snipe them and drink without breathing."

And subsonic bullets with a suppressed rifle meant he wouldn't get caught all that easily.

Ryan's eyes widened. "In all my life…I've never heard the like."

Me neither, for that matter. Most vamps relished the thrill, but this guy did it to survive. Vince glanced away, his jaw working.

"Come on," Ryan said. "Least I can do before going to ground is to help you get a reliable supply."

A restlessness ran through me. A sense that I've been away from Alya for too long. I turned toward Ryan's apartment block, frowning. I had to go back to her. It felt wrong to leave her in that apartment to fend for herself, especially now. She was lost. Confused. I was letting her get mixed up with Ryan for fuck's sake. I might as well have led her to the slaughter myself. Now Alick was loose in town. I needed to get back. My cell phone rang just as I started towards the apartment.

"Romano." Damn. I frowned at the screen, trying to decide what to do. Logic told me to just disappear, but I couldn't do that. He was my friend, and he'd already lost Vince. I answered. "Tyr—" I stopped short and pinched the bridge of my nose. "Parker."

I checked over my shoulder, and sure enough, my phone call had stopped Vince and Ryan from leaving too. We were a team now, so I put the phone onto speaker.

"Are you close to the office?" Romano asked, unaware. "We got a break in the plane crash."

Seriously? Now? I shook my head, preparing to tell him—truthfully—that I was on the wrong side of town. Ryan's expression stopped me. His brows knitted together as if trying to figure out what to do out of many more options than I was willing to entertain.

I just wanted to get back to Alya and make sure she was okay. But if I did that, I might miss out on some vital information on the rebels. Still, the whole thing made me nervous. I glanced in Alya's direction again.

Ryan's gaze focused on my face as he sensed out my feelings. Damn it. I used to be so careful.

"Nick?" Romano prodded.

"Just hang on a sec." I turned speaker phone off and

covered the mic. "She's alone there."

"I know." Ryan rubbed his jaw. "She'll be fine. No one will think someone's home." A sardonic smile flitted over his face. "They know me or they know of me, and it's a widely acknowledged fact that I have no heart. You need to stick around the FBI for as long as possible. So act normal."

I scowled. "If something happens—"

"Nothing will happen."

"While you're there, check that the griffs aren't on Romano's tail anymore," Vince said.

"Fine," I grumbled and put the phone to my ear. She'd be fine. Ryan was right. I was, once again, letting my emotions cloud the issue. Last time I did that, my whole life had gone to hell. "Romano?"

"Yeah. Something up?"

"Nah, it's nothing. I'll be right there."

I hung up and checked that my gun was safely holstered. Everything secured, I ran to the office.

RYAN

Vince and I walked into the hospital in silence. Maybe I was an idiot to let a vampire in, but Vince didn't really seem all that hungry. In fact, the moment we entered the lobby, he dropped into a chair and flopped open a newspaper. He didn't breathe. Luckily, we weren't sharing the lobby with accident or shooting victims. I stopped and watched him.

"See something interesting?" I asked.

Vince's grip on the paper tightened. "This is stupid. I'll just go get food the normal way."

"But this is much easier for you."

"Not safe," he said, nervously checking around him. "I was a cop in this precinct. People here knew me."

"We came all this way. Let's at least try."

"I was hoping for a faster employee turnover."

I glimpsed a female doctor about the same time as we caught her attention. Dr. Hartley was a nice woman. Pretty. From what I'd been told, she had a wonderful bedside manner. She walked over, folding her arms. I felt her sadness and pain right through the buzzing coming from the rest of the hospital. It was numbing, crushing. How did she manage to get up every day?

"Morning," she said, smiling brightly, defiant to it all. That impressed me. "What do we have here?"

I glanced in Vince's direction. From the horrified vibes coming my way, he obviously knew the pretty doctor. He'd sunken even deeper in his seat, hiding more of himself behind the paper.

"He's anemic," I said. "Needs a transfusion, but he's afraid of needles."

Vince slid off his chair and marched back outside, making damn sure to keep his head down. He flipped up his jacket's collar to hide more of his face.

"Walks well for an anemic needing a transfusion," she said, lifting an eyebrow.

"Titanic willpower."

She gazed out through the glass doors. Vince stood there waiting for me. His hands were thrust deep into his pockets, and his head hung. Her pain shot up by leaps and bounds—so intense I almost experienced it myself.

"Are you okay?" I asked.

She shook herself. "Oh, yes. Yes." The bright smile returned, but her pain only settled back slightly. "He reminds me of someone I once…knew." Her gaze went back to Vince. "It…it's sort of like seeing a ghost. I know I should stop looking, but…"

Vince could probably hear us. His shoulders bunched up as if he'd been burned, then he walked out of sight. Dr. Hartley's posture sagged and she released a sad little laugh. "Sorry. You must think I'm insane."

No, not really. Obviously, Dr. Hartley knew Vince. He had definitely recognized her.

"No," I said, "similar things have happened to me." Although granted, the people haunting me usually were alive. "Let me go talk to him. Have a good day." I gave her a reassuring smile, then left her standing there in the lobby.

I had to walk three blocks before Vince stepped out of an alleyway ahead of me.

"Thanks for your offer," he said, "but I've gotten along just fine so far."

"Who is she?"

"No one." He started to walk away again.

I followed, trying my best to ignore the pain my body picked up from him. It was hard to do when it more than rivaled Dr. Hartley's. "Right. She was pretty torn up about seeing you."

"Like I said, it was a bad idea." His jaw clenched. "She's my wife. Or was. She married someone else three years after I died."

I winced. "I'm sorry."

"You know what they say. Being a vampire sucks." The smile he flashed my way wasn't real.

"Why did you let me take you to the hospital if you knew she'd be there?"

His fake smile dropped away. "Fucked if I know. Maybe I wanted a glimpse of her close up. Or maybe I thought she wasn't there today. Or…" He sighed and rubbed the back of his neck. "One thing's for sure. I didn't expect her to walk right up to me."

Vince wasn't the only one risking a lot for a woman.

"So you're not going back there, are you?" I asked.

He shook his head. "Can't risk her spotting me again. I know her. At some point she'd walk up to me, trying to prove to herself that she's seeing things. And then, I'd have destroyed her life all over again."

"I'm truly sorry. I didn't know."

"It's okay," Vince said, patting my shoulder. "You

couldn't have. You weren't here when I was alive. I better go get something for lunch. Give me your number, so I can call you when I'm done."

I recited my number and he keyed it into his phone.

Vince glanced back toward the hospital one more time as he returned his phone to his pocket. "Everything happens for a reason, right?"

I didn't have an answer to that, but then, he didn't seem to expect one. He released a sad chuckle and drifted into an alley. Once out of sight, he shot off in search of food. I turned back to the hospital.

Better to let everyone think I had no reason to go back home just yet.

NICK

Air rushed over my body and tugged at my hair as I ran. Everything around me was quiet except for the wind whistling by. It was a peace I hadn't realized I missed, but no matter how much I wanted to enjoy it, my thoughts kept going back to Alya.

After a quick detour to my flat for a change of clothes, I stopped in an alley next to the FBI building. I straightened out my suit and ran my fingers through my hair to ensure it was mostly in place. Wouldn't do to look like I'd survived the inside of a tornado. Once presentable, I headed into the office.

A wall of noise and chaos brought me to a halt. I winced and waited for my body to readjust. Keen senses sucked when everything around me was almost too sharp to bear. I'd been playing the mortal for too long.

Romano approached me, frowning. "Do you have a hangover?" He held up the file.

"Maybe." I took the file from his hands and scanned over it. "Anonymous informant?"

"Yeah, he found me at the gym. Said I'd be intrigued by this address if I wanted to know what happened on the plane. Even mentioned the suspects walking off the crash site unharmed."

Oh no. Alick should have taken care of this. Our little

110

run-in must have prevented him from getting around to it. "You trust him?"

Romano shrugged. "He—I don't know. It just felt like he knew something."

"What did he look like?"

"Six foot four. Early to mid-twenties. Black hair, blue eyes."

Fuck. It sounded like Davenport. Looked like my luck had once again turned for the worst. Romano's keen eyes didn't miss my reaction, even when I was careful not to show my feelings.

"Are you sure you're okay?" he asked.

"Yeah. Why?"

He shrugged. "Dunno. I get the feeling something changed last night."

A lot had changed. And kept changing. In fact, this felt like being stuck on top of a mud slide.

"No, I'm fine." I skimmed the rest of the report.

The information was thin, neither confirming nor ruling out my suspicion. God, please let it not be Davenport. If there was ever a protector the griffons feared most, Davenport was it. He was fanatical in his hatred of us. With good reason. Ryan and I had killed his brother. In retaliation, he'd single-handedly captured and killed the strongest griffon he could find so he could drink the poor sod's blood—risking his life to become a protector. All to have the maximum chance of taking me and Ryan down.

We headed out in silence. Romano drove. I sat in the passenger seat, worrying about what we'd find. About what I'd do when we found it.

I closed my eyes and let my senses rove about,

searching for any griffons in the area. No use looking for protectors. They were always careful to mask their power to a near whisper. Even Davenport. And Aleria.

Did Davenport know she was alive? Probably not. Her automatic response had always been to mask her power, so not even the protectors would know she'd survived the crash unless they saw her. If—no, when—they figured out she'd been hospitalized, they'd find Ryan's report of her death. Ryan, who hadn't bothered to change his name.

Ryan, who up until his *very* recent change of mind, had been hunting Aleria almost obsessively for centuries.

Oh fuck. I should have thought of this sooner.

I had to assume they hadn't found the records yet, because when Davenport did, we'd have to deal with him personally. Would Alya even remember how much she despised him? Did she still despise him?

We stopped before a glass monolith similar to Ryan's building and I forced myself to concentrate on my present surroundings. Nothing felt untoward. In fact, no power stirred about me at all. It gave me the chills.

Davenport could be here, watching me walk into his trap. He'd recognize me instantly. I was a rogue, would anyone even bother to come if a pack of protectors ambushed me? I rolled my shoulders and entered the building, flashing my badge at the porter. He led us up to the floor Romano requested, and at our order he stayed by the elevator. We headed up the corridor, toward the number we were looking for.

Someone had dripped blood onto the handle and left the door ajar. How nice of them to keep us within the law. Filling out the paperwork for a search warrant had always been *such* a pain. A shiver ran down my spine.

Davenport was making this too easy.

Romano gave me a look and drew his gun. I followed suit and went in first, making sure all the rooms off the short hallway were clear. I reached the end of it and turned the corner. The sight greeting me made my hope sink to my shoes. I lowered the gun and just stared.

Two corpses hung upside down, throats slit, disemboweled and charred. Their power remained, soaking into me. The stench of burned flesh and hair hung thick in the room. Despite the window being open, smoke threw a haze over the gruesome scene. On the wall behind the corpses, written in blood, were the words *Griffon Scum*.

Davenport had been so kind as to nail a business card onto each corpse's forehead to help us identify them. These were the griffs who'd crashed the plane. Romano bent closer to examine the business cards. I gripped my hands behind my back and fought the urge to throw up. My worlds had crashed together and I didn't know what would be left at the end.

"What's that supposed to mean?" Romano asked, frowning at the message on the wall. "Gangs against terrorists?"

No. I knew very well what it meant. Davenport knew. He knew about Aleria's fake death, probably from torturing these two griffs. From there, he probably made enquiries on the air crash case and found me. He then drew his own conclusions. Especially if he found Ryan's records at the hospital.

Instead of attacking, he'd sent me this message. He specifically did it through my partner so I'd know how close he was. To make me extra aware of the fact that he could be coming up right behind me at any moment and I wouldn't know it.

This was his twisted method of getting revenge. He wanted me to look over my shoulder all the time until the real attack came.

I stared at the corpses, trying to figure out what to do now. I wanted to call Alick to come clean up the mess, but couldn't do that with Romano watching me.

Suddenly, a huge blast of life force hit me. I turned towards it instinctively, recognizing Alick behind it. Then I realized the direction it came from.

Alya.

I ran.

ALERIA

I paced in my room, waiting for the guys to come back. What if something had gone wrong? What if it had been a trap? Could griffons even be trapped by griffons? I ran my hand through my hair, shaking my head. I was being irrational, but I couldn't help myself. There was only one way to check. I dove into the small pile of belongings I'd brought from the hospital, searching for the business card Nick had given me.

I found it under a shoe, released a soft shout of glee, then shot to the telephone. I started tapping in the numbers, but stopped when the front door opened.

Power buffeted my back. Not Nick. Not Ryan. I slammed the receiver down and faced the intruder. The sight of his face seared a bright flash of pain through my head and I staggered back, putting distance between us.

This griffon was dangerous. Hundreds of little memories raced through my mind, featuring him killing the people I protected. I blinked and shook my head, trying to free up my thoughts to focus on the present. He gaped at me, as if initially shocked at my presence. A slow, leering grin appeared on his face, sending shivers cascading down my spine.

"Well, well," he said, skulking into the room. "This is a lovely surprise."

I slipped my hand into my pocket, squeezing Nick's lighter in my fist. "Wish I could say the same."

He closed the door. "You have no idea how long I've waited for this moment. The best part is, I won't have to share."

I tossed my head and pulled out the lighter, hiding it behind my back. Please, please, please let it be reliable. "Wouldn't want to disappoint," I said and sparked the lighter.

To my immense relief, the flame came to life. It was effortless to pull the fire into me. Second nature. My insides warmed and I dropped the lighter.

He stalked closer. "Here birdy, birdy."

I opened my hands, curling my fingers a little. With a tiny prompt of my will, two fireballs appeared in my palms. Not quite big enough, but then, the flame I'd started with was tiny. His leer faded and he paled. I threw both at him, aiming for his chest.

The fireballs impacted with small explosions, sending him flying back. I sprinted for the kitchen, lighting the oven and all of the stove's plates.

The griffon—Alick! That was his name. Alick roared in the sitting room. His power washed over me like a tidal wave, battering at my defenses. My heart hammered as I pushed back, fighting the draw he was trying to place on my soul. I needed to focus.

I placed my hands on the burning stove. The intense heat yanked my attention back to the fire. Hot fire. Blue flames. Lovely. This I could work with.

Alick burst into the kitchen. I vaulted over the counter and kicked him squarely in the face before landing. He staggered back, buying me more time. I drew in more fire, running for the supply cabinet. I grabbed a mop and sprinted for the fire alarm.

Alick grabbed me by the hair, yanking back with enough force to bring tears to my eyes. "Oh no you don't." He shoved his power against my defenses, trying to access my soul against my will.

Even though Alick wasn't as strong as Ryan, I'd buckle in a matter of minutes. I slammed the mop's handle to his temple. The wood snapped from the force of the hit. It infuriated him, but at least his focus was gone. I beat my head back against his face, earning a blistering curse and a slackening in my hair.

I scrambled away, gripping the broken mop in my hands. The fire alarm. I needed to deactivate it. I took aim and threw the mop like a javelin at the smoke sensor.

It hit home, shattering the unit.

Alick roared and dove into me from behind, slamming my body into the hard marble floors.

"So," he growled in my ear, pinning me down. "You're their dirty little secret. Why they didn't want to meet me here. Which one are you fucking? Or is it both?"

I narrowed my eyes. Let the idiot talk. He had no focus. First thing he should have done was turn off the stove. I drew in all the fire I could get. It warmed me like a mother's hug. It ran through my blood like lava.

I lit myself up like a roman candle, setting us both alight. His disadvantage: griffs don't do well with fire. Alick screamed and jerked away, rolling to kill the flames. I lit up the rest of the apartment, multiplying my power tenfold. The flames licked at the marble tiles as if I'd poured kerosene on them. Nothing could kill the flames now. Only me.

Alick screamed, his rolling growing frantic.

I made the flames white hot. "I'm pretty sure I warned you about attacking me," I said, watching. The cloying stench of burning hair and flesh invaded my nostrils. God, I hated this.

"Mercy!" he wailed. "I beg you!"

I couldn't go through with it. For some reason I couldn't explain, I kept myself from killing him. I sighed and let the flames drift off him while I headed for the bedrooms. Maybe there was something important I should save. Suddenly, Alick's power came at me again. When I turned, I found him on his feet and glaring at me. His jaw clenched and he pressed his power against my defenses again.

I snarled and grabbed the first thing at hand—a kitchen chair—and hurtled it at him feet first. The force of my throw pinned him to the wall opposite me. His power instantly faded.

His chest rattled. The flames grew white hot as I summoned all of the blaze's heat to me, watching him. He leaned his head back against the wall, blood dribbling out of his mouth. This time, he requested no mercy. Just as well, because I had none left to spare him.

"Ali, no!"

Ryan.

I closed my eyes. "Walk away," I commanded. He couldn't come too close.

"Please," he said, moving up behind me. I flinched back, afraid of burning him. "Don't. You're better than this."

There was no threat from him. Even as I felt his draw, I knew it was different. Alick was about greed, Ryan was about protecting me. Still, he shouldn't be this close. Not while I was in full power.

"Please," he said again, taking another step closer. If he came any nearer, he'd die just from proximity. I was burning too hot for any griffon to survive. His face was set with pain already. How was he withstanding this?

"Stop," I said. "You need to move away."

"Think, Ali. You hate killing. Don't do this."

How did he know? Was it a lucky guess? Because he was right. Even now, the thought of killing Alick repulsed me. Still, I swallowed and focused on Alick. The faster I took him out, the sooner things would be safe for Ryan.

"No!" Ryan rushed me and pressed his hand to my cheek, forcing me to look at him instead. His skin sizzled. I could smell it burning. "Ali..." He gasped in pain. His skin blistered and he collapsed.

I cried out and let go of the fire, catching Ryan as he fell. My whole body was shaky, giving way under his weight.

"Ryan!" I shouted, but nothing happened. Only Alick's eternal death rattle reached my ears.

Then I felt it, a feeble pull. *Ryan*. I held onto him, closing my eyes. After everything he had done to protect me I couldn't let him die. I closed my eyes and opened my defenses, basically handing over my soul. My life drained out of me. First slowly, then faster as his power grew. Once it started, it wouldn't stop. I caressed his face, watching the blisters fade away as he healed. Hopefully he'd understand that this was a gift; that he wouldn't have to feel guilty.

RYAN

Every single instinct told me to wake up. My strength grew by leaps and bounds. The rush was incredible. Nothing rivaled it. This euphoria could only come from claiming a protector.

No. What had I done? I groaned and fought to stop the draw. Ali lay on top of me. Limp. Could it be too late? I sobbed, finally managing to master myself.

My true nature snarled at me for interrupting, but I disregarded its urgings. Ali's life force sustained me, healing me, but I couldn't take it. I wouldn't.

I put my arms around her, sensing out the connection between us. Usually, the bond between me and a phoenix felt like a vacuum, tearing the life out of someone despite any resistance I might have found. This felt different, like a bridge joining me to her. Her life flowed over to me with no resistance. I could feel her emotions, the sensation of me holding her and how much she liked it when I did.

My heart hammered and I swallowed. This…this was unknown. No protector ever gave up their souls willingly. I knew that. God knew I'd stolen enough souls to know the difference. But this was one soul I didn't want. Well…actually I did. Just not at the cost of her. The thought of losing her filled me with dread.

My true nature shouted at me, telling me I was an idiot. I didn't care. I had to do something to save her, something that might return her to life. I kissed her forehead and focused on finding her inside me. It wasn't all that hard. Everything beautiful and warm was her. Anything feeling like an impending disaster was me.

I shoved her life force back across the bridge between us, into her, its rightful place. She let me.

Her heart rate picked up and her vibrancy returned. I did my best to shut down the connection between us— just in case either of us changed our mind. The ghost of a connection remained despite my best efforts. I felt her the same way I felt any griffon.

I shook myself and sat up, holding her close. It had to be some warped sort of wishful thinking from me. She'd practically lit up the apartment and had been in full command of her power. There was no way she could have hidden so much power. In fact, I'd felt her when battling Alick. Griffons could have felt her for miles. But right now she was too weak to project power. How could I still feel her?

I grew vaguely aware of Nick approaching. He was there when I turned my head.

"What happened?" he demanded, crouching down next to me. "I came as fast as I could."

Pain etched his features, but for some reason, his anger didn't seem to be focused at me. That was new.

"Alick must have been curious," I said. "I found him there," I nodded to where Alick was still pinned. He'd be there, forever dying until one of us freed him. "She was going to kill him."

"And you…"

"Almost died stopping her. And now—" I swallowed down the emotion threatening to drown me and looked at Aleria's serene face. "You feel her, don't you?"

"No."

I frowned at him. "But—" I still did. Like she was part of me. "She's alive."

Nick exhaled heavily, as if he'd held his breath. "Fuck, that's a relief. Okay, you take care of her. I'll get rid of him." He jerked his head in Alick's direction.

Vince came in and whistled. "Never a dull moment. I go hunt for an hour and I miss everything. I'll say this, though. Your lady sure kicks ass." He poked at Alick's chest. "Makes me think it'd have been kinder to shoot him in the eye."

Alick tried to growl, but it came out as a rattling sound. He coughed up blood. Drops of it rolled down his chin.

"Anyway," Vince said. "We better get going. I crossed paths with one badass looking phoenix on the way here. I think he's going to kill any griff he finds. Just waiting for his back-up to show up."

Nick winced. "Black hair, blue eyes, six foot four?"

"Yeah. You know him?"

"Davenport."

Shit. This definitely wouldn't look good. "We need to get out of range and fast."

Nick nodded. "Go. Call me when you're safe. I'll bring your supplies."

I picked Ali up and stumbled out of my apartment. Where the hell was I supposed to go? The protectors could be anywhere. A sudden flare of heat burned through my thoughts. I winced and checked on Ali, but she didn't cause it. She sensed the heat with tranquility. The protectors were letting her know they were near. Okay. Things were getting weird, but maybe I could locate them this way.

It wouldn't be comfortable for me. I focused on the intensifying heat as more protectors powered up. Now that I felt them, locating them wasn't different to me sensing out other beings. They weren't far at all, but they were only coming from one side. About twenty blocks away to the west.

I held Ali closer and shot into the sky. Luckily for us both, I had a place where no one would ask questions, and it was on the opposite side of the city.

Hotel Beaufort was one of the best hotels in existence. I'd always assumed someone from the Firm would eventually find me, so I kept a suite there, just in case. I landed us in the alley, then went in.

The concierge's eyebrows shot up at the sight of me carrying a prone woman. As if he didn't have a dirty little secret of his own. He needed to take off once a month so he could howl at the moon.

"My suite," I said, forgoing small talk in favor of speed. "I expect two more, so book two more rooms to my name."

"Y-yes sir," he said, exactly as soft-spoken as I remembered him. "Would you like something to eat?"

"Just someone to let me in."

"Of course." He summoned one of the bellhops and started typing.

Ali stirred softly, whimpering. I hushed her and kissed her brow. It felt like the right thing to do, even when my true nature snarled.

The bellhop beckoned me and I followed him into the elevator. When we reached the top floor, we exited and he opened the suite's door. He set the key down on the table and then stood waiting expectantly.

I sighed. "I have nothing on me right now. But I'll arrange for the tip later."

Maybe I wore a forbidding expression, or maybe it was the fact that I'd simply been given the key to the most expensive suite in the hotel, but the bellhop smiled.

"Of course, sir. Have a wonderful day."

He left us and I took Ali to the bedroom. She needed rest, but I just wasn't ready to let her go. So I lay down with her and held her tight.

ALERIA

I sobbed and opened my eyes. It was dark, but strong arms held me, keeping me safe. Ryan. I burrowed closer to his chest, trying to deal with the profound sense of loss I'd just experienced. Ryan's hold on me tightened.

"What is it, Ali?" he asked gently. His fingers caressed my cheek, wiping my tears.

I sniffled. "I dreamed of my parents. I know why I came to New York."

He shifted closer, drawing me to him a bit more, comforting me. "Is it bad?"

"Yes." I fought back my tears, but they escaped anyway. "My parents. They wanted this death to be their last. I was supposed to be there. I was…supposed…" I sobbed harder, pressing my face to his chest. My father chose to die with my mother this time. They wouldn't start another life cycle.

"Oh Ali." He held me as I cried, caressing my back and shoulders.

"I lost them. I'll never see them again."

Ryan kissed my forehead. "I'm sorry," he murmured. "I can't imagine how that must feel."

I shook my head. "It hurts. Like they died just now."

"Could they still be alive?"

"I-I don't know."

"If they were still alive, would you know how to find them?"

I wracked my thoughts, trying to remember anything that could be useful. Nothing came to me. My hope sank deeper and I cried more, shivering. "Nothing. I don't...know."

"It's okay," he said, squeezing me. "Don't be scared. It'll come back to you. One day."

"But why? Why can't I just remember?"

"You will." He tenderly nudged my chin up, then kissed the tip of my nose. "I know it's difficult, but you need to be patient with yourself."

Something about him just calmed me. I relaxed into him, sighing. When I did, something else struck me. "I'm...alive."

"Yes," Ryan said softly. "And safe. Alick won't come close to you with me here."

I shuddered at the reminder. "I could have killed you."

"Ditto," he said. It was too dark to see his face without me accessing my power, but I sensed his frown from his tone of voice. "You shouldn't have given your life away like that."

"Better that than me killing you."

"Why?" His body tensed against mine.

I shrugged. "It would have hurt, seeing you die because of something I did."

"Hurt?" he shouted, pulling away. "Do you have any idea about how hard I've worked not to hurt you? And then you basically begged me to do the opposite!" He grasped my shoulders. "I'd never be able to forgive myself—"

"Why not?" I shot back, sitting up. "You know I

offered my life. You wouldn't have stolen it—"

"Because I care about you!"

We both stilled. The words reverberated between us. "You care…" I cupped his jaw.

"Yes. I don't know how, but I can't stand the thought of harming you. Of you coming to any harm."

Suddenly, it made sense. He protected me because he cared. Not because of some promise he'd made to someone else, but because I was important to him. It was a heady realization fraught with danger, but I wanted it. I wanted to be there with him, in his arms.

"I'm sorry," I whispered, splaying my fingers over the cotton covering his chest and snuggling up to him once more. "I didn't realize."

"You weren't supposed to." His voice was gruff, but his touch was soft as silk as he trailed his fingers down my arm. He covered my hand with his. "It's not really…normal."

I smiled and shook my head. "No, but maybe that's what makes it special. This idea of me and you. Well…" I mulled it over for a few seconds. "You beat your dark side to care for me, and I somehow managed to trust you enough to care as well."

He leaned in and kissed me gently, giving me a chance to change my mind. I didn't. Didn't even want to. I slipped my arm around his side, drawing myself nearer to him. It was all he needed. To know I was sure. Once he had that certainty, he deepened the kiss, slanting his mouth over mine. His body tensed, slowly, like a coiling spring. There was so much energy he held back.

He whispered against my lips. "I'm in trouble."

"Oh?"

"I could hurt you."

"You won't," I said and pecked his lips. "Maybe if you relax a little."

His laugh was breathy, but it worked. He stole a little kiss, his draw lightly tugging at my soul. It didn't feel dangerous, though. It felt right. I touched his lips, giving in to him, sensing my soul nestling with his as if we were one person. I gasped softly. The feeling was thrilling. Exhilarating.

Ryan moaned my name and muttered something in a language I didn't understand. He kissed me again, but this was different. Closer to the second time we'd kissed. Raw. Primal. My heart thundered. My stomach felt hollowed out. I turned onto my back, drawing him with me. It felt so good, I moaned against his lips, begging for more.

His touch seared my skin under my shirt, then the air cooled me when he pulled my shirt off. His hand roved down my sides, spanned my abdomen while his tongue engaged mine in a wicked sort of ritual. I moaned again, wanting to feel him beneath my fingers too. I all but ripped his shirt off. I breathed with relief to be in contact with the heat of his body. I caressed his back, letting his muscles play and stretch under my fingers.

He hummed softly, encouraging me to explore more. It was a surprise, though. I'd expected flawlessness, but instead discovered a variety of scars. His body was perfection anyway. Ryan trailed kisses down my neck, his fingers working my bra loose. Once he'd released the clasp, he slipped it down over my arms, making sure to touch every inch of skin along the way. I whimpered softly, pulling his face towards mine once more. He

128

obliged, pressing his body to mine as we kissed. At the same time, he worked my jeans loose and pulled them down with my underwear. Once he'd tossed them aside, he stroked my thigh before resting his hand on my hip.

We didn't say anything, just breathing away a few moments, waiting for something. The whole time, his body pressed against mine, the contact burning me, marking me. But then he claimed my mouth again and worked his own trousers off. I moaned and helped him, keeping him close. He rested on his elbows and cupped my face between his hands, then kissed me with a deep yearning. I held him tight, wrapping myself around him. And then we were one, body and soul. He wasn't gentle and I didn't care.

Our movements were hard, demanding more, driving us on, fusing us closer. Our moans and breaths mingled into our kisses. It was heaven mixed with torture, relentlessly taking me up, up, higher and higher until it felt like he'd claimed my soul again. I cried out, clinging to him, letting pure, white hot pleasure wash over me as he moved. He moaned my name, his body tensing while he emptied out into me. I sighed in bliss and he kissed me, so softly. He held me while we caught our breaths.

RYAN

I held Ali close, listening to her sleep. Her arm spanned my chest and her thigh rested across my hips. Long locks of hair spread out in all directions as her head rested lightly on my shoulder. The feel of her body near mine filled me with serenity. I tucked some fly-away tendrils behind her ear, exposing her face. I reached over and gently traced the shape of her lips with my thumb. They were swollen from our kisses. Ripened for more.

My cell phone rang, shattering my peace. Ali's brows furrowed, but she didn't wake, so I shifted until I could pull it out from my discarded jeans' pocket. She mumbled sleepily and snuggled closer to me.

I didn't recognize the number, but answered anyway, in case it was Nick or Vince. "Ryan."

"Blake," my father corrected. A habit he'd had for centuries. "Don't hang up," he commanded.

I winced, really wanting to disobey, but I had an ancient habit of following my father's orders. I didn't have to be nice about it, though. "What?" I snapped.

"Seems you keep strange company. I felt the little skirmish going on at your apartment."

I went cold. The words themselves and his tone sounded nonthreatening, but him speaking of it at all made me shudder inside. Ali opened her eyes and watched me, brows drawn together in puzzlement. I put my arm around her, fighting to stay calm for her sake.

"Who I keep company with has nothing to do with any of you," I said. Ali cupped my jaw, her frown deepening.

To my immense surprise, my father sighed. "You're right."

Really? Iron bands seemed to clasp around my chest. I tensed, trying to escape the feeling, but it didn't help. "What do you want?"

"Just to talk to you. Alick said you're not coming back."

My grip on the phone tightened. The hard plastic bit into my palm. "Is this your way of threatening me? Because I promise you, if any of your Firm members come near Aleria again, I'll take them out myself. I will demolish you and everything you've built."

I didn't wait for his reply. I hissed out a breath and smashed the phone, making sure the SIM card shattered with it. Ali didn't say anything. Instead she pulled closer, rubbing my chest gently, unknowingly easing my discomfort. I closed my eyes and focused on taking some deep breaths.

"Feels like everything's trying to break me," I whispered. Where did that come from?

"Even me?" she asked.

"Especially you. If something happened to you...I don't know."

Her finger pressed to my mouth, silencing my concerns. I sighed and pressed a kiss to my hand.

She smiled softly. "We'll figure something out." Her kiss was sweet, intoxicating.

I drew her closer, wanting a deeper taste. She came willingly, easily sliding onto my hips, pressing her chest to mine as she explored my mouth. A low groan escaped from somewhere deep inside me.

Ali pulled back and looked at me with heavily lidded eyes. Then she took me into her, slowly, as if claiming possession of me. God, if she knew how much she had already. I gripped her hips and drove deeper. Her back arched and she gasped, firing my blood up even more. We moved together, melding our bodies, rushing each other to completion. When we finished we collapsed onto the bed together, wholly wrapped up with each other.

Right then, no one else existed. It was just me and her, gently rocking, breathing heavily to recover from our passion. I held her in my arms, fighting the intrusion of the outside world.

But no matter what I did, my conscience couldn't be stilled. What was I doing? She trusted me to keep her safe, but I was endangering her with every second I stayed close. I couldn't let go, though. Couldn't fight the thought that the best place for her was wherever I was.

Was it really, though? And then, there were the secrets I kept. What would happen if she found out the wrong thing at the wrong time?

Would I be able to convince her to trust me past a certain point?

What would I do if I failed?

NICK

My sleep would have sucked if I had managed to sleep at all. I couldn't sleep a wink, even though I was in my own bed. Not when I'd spent the whole time worrying about Alya. Had she woken up? Was she even alive? Ryan hadn't phoned me yet, which worried me.

Alick was in the next room, slowly healing on the bits of power I fed him. As soon as he could walk on his own, I'd drop him off in the middle of nowhere to fend for himself. In the meantime, I had to wait for Ryan, since he'd moved too far out of range to sense.

I sat up and smoked while watching my clock's digits pace their way to 6 a.m. Vince had said he'd be by with coffee for me. I ran my hand through my hair.

If Alya had woken up, we'd need to figure out a way to get her to the protectors. Explaining her to the Firm was a bit much for Ryan and me to handle on top of all the other shit going on. The only way I'd ever really been sure she was safe from griffons was when she was with me. I'd forced myself to walk away when she'd learnt to hate me, but it made me want to die. I didn't know if I could ever do it again. And I'd have to, if she went to the protectors. The hatred between our kinds ran too deep.

Fuck. If only I'd convinced her to marry me.

The doorbell rang just as my alarm went off. Good old

Vince. I shuffled to the door, rubbing my face. My stubble felt coarse under my palm. Screw it, let it grow. Who was I trying to impress anyway? In the nanosecond before I opened the door, it struck me that whoever was on the other side was human.

Romano stood before me, wearing the scowl he reserved only for the suspects he nailed to the wall. Oh damn, I couldn't deal with this right now. And the asshole didn't even have coffee. I glanced over his shoulder, checking to see if Vince was around. There was no sign of the vamp. That was good, but I needed to get rid of Romano before he arrived.

"You look like hell." Romano shoved his way past me. He went straight to the kitchen and turned on the coffee machine.

Fucking A. I trudged in after him. "Hey, listen. I uh, have a visitor over—"

"Cut the crap, Nick." Romano pinned me with his best bad-cop stare. "I need you to tell me how deep in you are."

What? I shook my head as if I'd gotten water into my ear. "What exactly am I supposed to be *in*?"

"Terrorism. Murder. Conspiracy."

My stomach did a rough tumble. "Me? Come on. Romano. You're my friend. You know I don't—"

"I know *you* wouldn't, but I need to know how they got to you. Was it Blake Ryan? Because I've been seeing connections to everything big that's been happening lately, and they're tying you up nice and neat for a conviction."

Oh shit. Shit, shit, shit!

"First cop at the arson scene was plain clothes, Nick.

He saw you leave with a seriously injured man. Soon after that, there was an explosion." He narrowed his eyes. "*It was Ryan's flat, Nick,*" he said, punctuating his statement with a pointing finger. "I checked. Had to do some serious digging though. There were a lot of empty shell companies and shit to wade through. So what is he? A drug dealer? Strong man?"

I dropped into a chair and had to laugh at that. "Dean, stop. Seriously. Stop."

"You've been covering for these bastards all along!" Romano exploded at me.

I rubbed my face with both hands. I was too exhausted to lie. "Dean, why do you think I'm covering for them?"

"'Griffon Scum!'" he roared back at me. "Remember? The two terrorists? Well the same message was on Ryan's wall. Done in fire with some sort of unknown accelerant. Oh God. Is that a threat?"

Sure it was. To me and to Ryan, but Romano couldn't know about it. "No. No it's not. It's just—" Fuck it. Both my worlds were crumbling. Why bother? I checked on Alick through our power bond, then glanced back at Romano. Alick had passed out the moment I pulled the barstool out of him, and he was still out of commission. I sighed and sat forward. "Okay. I admit it. I'm in way over my fucking head, but Romano, you're better off not knowing how."

"Start talking or I'm putting you under arrest."

Fucking hell. Why did it have to come to this? I shrugged and leaned back in my chair. "Fine, but you better forget this the moment I've finished talking. Or you and I are both dead." I watched him, but he seemed unimpressed. "I'm a griffon. Have been my whole life, and will remain one until the day I die. Which…isn't any time soon. My real name is Prince Nikolai Yurevich Tyrov. I was born in Moscow in 1256. My mother was a mortal. My father wasn't. I got his genes. Ryan's my half-brother."

Romano's swarthy face went gray. "You're insane."

I held up my hand. We'd talk about my sanity soon enough. "There are two types of true immortals: griffons and phoenixes. Griffons can live for a fucking long time, but we have to kill phoenixes to live forever. Then there are the phoenixes who drink griffon blood in order to turn into protectors. They pretty much kill any griffon coming within range of their wards.

"The worst of all the protectors is on a killing spree because Ryan went and faked Aleria Tyson's death, so he could sneak her out of the hospital without the griffons knowing. She's a protector, and their chief's daughter, so you can see why they'd be a bit pissed at us. We don't talk, and they assumed either me or him killed her for her power.

"In the meantime, the Firm, a griffon organization that makes your idea of the Illuminati look like a playpen, is falling apart. As a result, two griffs went and took down the plane because their faction don't feel like hiding their immortality anymore.

"The Firm wants Ryan and me to clean up their huge ass mess, which is why Alick showed up, and indirectly why he's in my spare room recovering from a meeting with a high-speed barstool. Thrown by Aleria by the way, who is alive and well and who'd set the place on fire with her mind in order to match his power. So yeah, I'm in deep, and I probably won't be getting out of it any time soon."

Romano gaped at me through the whole thing.

"Two more things," I said. "Drinking our blood turns people into vampires, and my telling you all this is treason. If you tell anyone about this, a griffon will be dispatched to kill you. From what I've seen, it's not a pleasant way to go."

Romano shook his head, reaching for his service pistol. "You're insane."

I tilted my head, preparing to take the gun out of the equation. I was so not in the mood to be shot. "No, I'm not."

"Then you're lying. Because none of that is even remotely possible. You're under arrest."

The pistol slid against his holster as he drew. I was next to Romano before he could take aim. I grabbed his hand and twisted it, pressing his trigger finger back until he had no hope of shooting. Then I took the gun with my other hand.

Romano blinked. "Resisting arrest—"

I had to roll my eyes. "What can you do about it?"

His face grew hard. "How did you—"

"Griffons have powers superior to pretty much anything else in the world." I tucked his gun into my waistband and walked over to the coffee maker. It gurgled softly, squeezing out the last few drops of earthy, brown liquid.

Wait. *Coffee*.

"Uh, Dean? You might want to reconsider that," Vince said.

I glanced his way and found him leaning against the kitchen door, cup of joe in hand and shades still covering his eyes.

Romano stood frozen, bent over in an attempt to retrieve his second gun from his ankle holster. "You… You're…dead."

"Undead." Vince scowled and shifted his sunglasses onto the top of his head.

I went over and grabbed the steaming paper cup from him. "Give me that. What took you so long?"

He shrugged. "I heard him from the next block. It was a bit of a dilemma to me."

Romano managed to close his mouth. "But—" He staggered to one of my kitchen chairs and dropped into it. "How can this be real?"

I took a sip of the scalding hot coffee. At least it didn't look like Dean wanted to shoot me anymore. In fact, he looked more ready to keel over than anything else.

"That's a bit of a long story to tell right now," I said. "Breathe, Romano."

Romano gasped a breath and shook his head. His eyes glazed over with unshed tears.

"Dude," Vince said. "Lighten up. You're making me feel bad."

"Sorry," Romano whispered. "Just a lot to take in."

"I know," I said, "but I want you to realize we never did anything to harm you or any other mortal. In fact, that's the opposite of everything I've been trying to do ever since the crash. I've been trying to protect you."

"Yeah," Romano said, but his gusto had left him. I poured him a coffee and handed it over. He stared into the cup as if he didn't know what to do with it.

"Drink," I commanded. He obeyed mechanically. "Now that you know, will you help us?"

Romano suddenly burst out laughing and took a sip of coffee. Excellent. At least he was back to being himself. Even if he kept slipping glances to Vince, trying to convince himself that he wasn't hallucinating. "How can I possibly do that?"

"Obviously the Firm isn't so effective at keeping our business out of the mortal realms. We need you to do it for us."

Vince grimaced. "Only way to do that is to hack into the FB-freaking-I's system and mark the case as solved."

"Won't work," Romano said. "Our boss will know something's up. We know the 'terrorists' were murdered, but the case of who killed them is too high profile to just make it disappear. He's thinking about putting together another task force"

"Don't tell me," I said, practically inhaling the last of my coffee. "Press got wind of it."

"You got it."

I bit into the paper cup and waited for the caffeine to kick in so I could think. It didn't make much of a difference now that I didn't inject myself with morphine. Damn.

"They're crying 'serial killer,' now that the second 'Griffon Scum' message went up."

"No one died the second time," Vince pointed out.

Romano just gave him a bitter smile. "Since when did that stop the press?"

"Okay," I said. "So the case can't disappear. You need to stall for time. Hog the case for as long as you can. Investigate. Follow all relevant leads. Except the one leading to us. I'll figure out a way for us to get out of this mess."

"Are you coming in to work?"

It broke my heart, but I shook my head. "Too risky. Everyone and their mother can track me down to the FBI now."

"Then what the heck do I do with the new partner I'll get when you're gone?" Romano scowled. "And just when I'd house trained you too."

Crap. He had a point. "Keep him busy with other stuff."

"If he's any good, it won't work for long."

I knew that, but the only options we had to protect our secret were flimsy at best while the Firm was scrambling to stay standing. I crushed the paper cup and tossed it into my dustbin. "We just need it to work long enough for us to figure out what to do. Because whatever happens, we *can't* let the mortals find out about us."

Vince nodded. "Trust me. Vampirism doesn't suit humans."

Romano glanced between us, then nodded. "I'll do my best. What will you two do in the meantime?"

"We'll go underground almost as soon as you leave."

"Okay." He stood, then frowned. "But you're on record now as a person of interest in the murder case. If you run, it'll look like you're guilty."

"I know. Especially since I can't exactly hand in a resignation letter. But what other choice do I have?"

ALERIA

I woke up alone, with nothing to prove last night happened, save for the cool air caressing my skin and the indented pillow where Ryan had slept. The faint scent of his body lingered on me. I closed my eyes and inhaled, savoring it, then sat up and looked around. His clothes were gone.

The pastel walls and silver carpets should have given me a sense of peace. Instead, the room's sheer size and silence made me jumpy. Where was Ryan? I looked around and found a folded note propped up against a Japanese vase on the table opposite the bed. I picked it up and read.

Ali,
Went to get us supplies. Didn't want to wake you, but I won't be long anyway.
Don't leave the hotel.
Ryan

I frowned at the note, then put it back onto the table. This wasn't how I liked to wake up after a night of passion, although something told me it was far from the first time I had. It felt odd, thinking like this. Knowing and not knowing. Guessing at knowledge without any substantiation except for instinct.

My heart ached and I rubbed at the spot on my chest. It was so stupid. I didn't even know what made me sad. I needed to clear my head.

Snagging up my clothes, I dragged my feet to the shower. The hot water and steam did wonders to beat the melancholy out of me, but some fragment of it remained. I couldn't let myself worry about it, or I'd stop functioning. Right now, I needed to keep going like everything was normal. I stepped out of the shower and used one of the hotel's fluffy towels to dry myself. I got dressed, but the sooty smell in my clothes undermined the effect I was going for.

Things *weren't* normal. The guys hadn't told me what was going on, but I could sense it. My instincts told me Alick hadn't been there for me. He had been in search of Ryan or Nick. If I hadn't been there, one of them wouldn't have survived. Something was wrong.

Something serious. Something I needed to know.

I finger combed my hair, sparking another sense of deja vu. And a sense that Nick would move up behind me at any moment. His arms would encircle my waist and he'd rain kisses to my neck and shoulders. The memory felt so real, I closed my eyes and shivered, tilting my head.

"Marry me," he said, nipping at my earlobe. "We'll run away together."

The memory vanished before I knew the answer. I about faced, but only fading steam spread around me. Why Nick, and why after Ryan and I had slept together? I knew there'd been something between us, but marriage?

Why hadn't he told me?

I hugged myself to ward off chills running up my

arms, then raced out of the room, barely stopping to grab a key card.

The ghosts of my memories followed me. I sprinted down the corridor and into the elevator. When the door closed, Luc faced me in my reflection. He silently accused me of something I couldn't remember, growing larger with every second. I cried out and punched the button for the ground floor.

This was stupid. I shook my head and forced myself to face my reflection again. This time it was only me, dressed in a sooty t-shirt and jeans. The elevator slowly descended, trapping me with reflections at every angle.

I needed out. Even though I couldn't see him, it felt as if Luc was still there. Watching me. Resenting me. Why? Because of Ryan? Nick? Shivers shot over me again. The elevator stopped and opened at the ground floor. I fled into the lobby. The glass front door beckoned me, but I remembered Ryan's message. After my run-in with Alick, I didn't want to do anything that one of the guys might see as a risk.

Luc suddenly appeared out of the crowd passing by, facing me, his eyes wide in astonishment. "*Aleria?*" he mouthed, completely agog.

I shuddered, taking a step back. Something wasn't right. I couldn't place it, but this wasn't right. He didn't smile. Luc always smiled. No matter how surprised he was, his smile would take over the moment he saw me.

A blinding pain lanced through my brain and everything went black.

"Aleria?" Luc whispered, waking me up. He was sneaking into my room through the bay window, looking almost exactly the same as when he'd left.

"Have you lost your mind?" I hissed, grabbing up my covers. My sleeping clothes were so sheer. I might as well have been naked.

A grin brightened his face. "Just thought I'd visit first thing."

I glowered at him and lurched for my night gown. "What makes you think I even want to see you?" I whispered, satisfied to see the smile fade. "You left *for ten years*. No goodbye. No nothing."

"I'm sorry," he said, drooping his head, but peeking up enough to meet my gaze. "That was inexcusable."

"Get out," I said, yanking on my gown while coming to a stand. "The maids will be here any moment."

"Not before I've talked to you," he said and went to the door. He locked it and took out the key.

Anger drove me straight to him. I tried to grab the key from him, but he held it out of reach. "Get out," I repeated.

"Al, I did it. I took the blood. I'm like you now." The grin returned.

I stared at him, not comprehending. When I did, I was furious. "You took the blood?" I ground out past the fury threatening to choke me. "Without telling me?"

"I needed to do it. For us to be together."

I reeled, then I shoved him with enough force for him to hit the door with a thud. Let the maids hear it. And let them just dare comment on it. "How dare you make such a decision—"

"I did it for you," he said, reaching for me.

I shoved at his chest. "No, you did it for you. If you'd done anything for me, it would have been *not* becoming a protector!"

"Al, *ma chère*…" He grabbed my arms and held me firm while I struggled. But I had the superior experience. I used it to slam his body to the floor. He held on to me, though, pulling me down with him. My body fell onto his.

"Don't '*ma chère*' me, you bastard!" I slapped him wrist first, aiming to hurt. My heart had just broken. It was only fair that I shared the pain.

Luc grunted and rolled us over, trying to pin me, but I was too fast and hit repeatedly into his stomach and chest, kicking at his legs with mine. Soon, I'd have purchase to get back on top and when I did, he'd get all hell.

He leaned in, something no one else would do. He knew I wouldn't knife him in the back. Gently, he caught my wrists and pinned them above my head. He nuzzled my cheek softly, giving me a chance to catch my breath. Instead of abating, the gusts turned into sobs.

I couldn't help it nor hold in the pain he'd inflicted.

"Hush, *chère*," he murmured, releasing my hands to caress my dampened cheeks. "Everything's fine now."

"No," I wailed, "it'll never be fine. Now I'll lose you."

He shook his head, then rested it against mine. "No. That's why I did this. So we could live together. I'll be reborn less often. You won't have to be alone so much."

"No!" I shouted. "Don't you see? You'll die. Forever! We all do at some stage."

"That's your fear?" He lifted his head, showing me his beaming smile. "So you love me."

"Of course I fucking love you, you idiot!" I really

145

should have qualified that, because I only had chance to take a breath before his mouth claimed mine, demanding I show him.

I wanted to. Really, I wanted to. For the tiniest of moments, my judgment slipped and I savored his taste. It was wrong of me. I loved Nick. But I'd loved Luc long before that. In a way that should never have been requited.

It was wonderful in a terrible way, both a great gift and a severe punishment. I couldn't let it go on, but he held me captured between his body and the floor. I whimpered, forcing myself to turn my head. "Luc…"

My gaze caught Nick crouched on my window seat. He must have risked flying in to come see me. His face was a mask of rage. Oh God no.

"Don't stop on my account," he drawled, letting his power grow. This was madness! Giving his position away to any protector in the area.

I gasped, wanting to tell him to stop, but Luc was on his feet in a flash, drawing power from the fading embers in my fireplace.

Nick grinned, eyes emotionless. "Not yet, hatchling. I'll kill you once you have power worth my time."

Luc growled. "Why not try now?" He lifted his hands, aiming for Nick. A deep red ball of flame appeared at his palms.

I screamed and launched myself at Luc, pushing his arms down. "No!" One of them would definitely die if Luc let his fire loose. The blood Luc had taken must have been so powerful, but Nick had superior experience and rage on his side.

Nick's mocking laughter tore at me. "Come find me,

146

hatchling, when you don't have a Strongblood protecting you."

When I turned to the window, he was gone. I sagged to my knees, feeling as if he'd taken my heart with him. He wouldn't be back. Everything I'd trusted him with, all the dreams we'd built together... I'd shattered them in a moment's time.

"Alya," Nick said, shaking me gently. "Wake up."

He was back? It couldn't be, not after I'd betrayed him like that.

"I'm sorry. So sorry." I gathered my strength and sat up, throwing my arms around his neck, pressing my face to the hollow there I knew so well. "I'm sorry…"

"Alya…" He sounded defeated. "Wake up. You're in New York now."

New York? I pried my eyes open, focusing on the hotel's luxurious décor, the crowd gathering around me. The bystanders' hushed whispers brought me to myself more. New York. I peeked over Nick's shoulder at the glass doors.

No Luc.

I burrowed my head in his neck again, seeking calm. "I thought I saw Luc."

He stiffened. "Davenport was here?"

"What happened?" Ryan demanded before I had time to answer. His strong arms drew me away from Nick and lifted me off the cold marble floors.

"Davenport found us," Nick said. "She fainted."

Ryan started walking. "I have a cab."

"Good."

I rested my head on Ryan's shoulder, chewing my lip. It felt good to have his strength. But deep down, I wished Nick had put his arms around me. To have known that I was forgiven.

NICK

I opened the cab door and let Ryan and Alya climb in first. When I followed, I found him cradling her to his torso, pressing a kiss to her hair. I clamped my jaw as tight as I could and slammed the door shut.

"Where to?" the cabby asked.

A gunshot went off and all the pedestrians ducked. The cabby stepped on the gas.

I searched the sky-scrapers' tops. Vince must have made an effort to make a noise so we'd know he'd run into at least one protector. Odds were the shot wouldn't kill whoever it was aimed at, but it would keep the protector busy long enough for us to get away. We needed to figure out how to talk to Davenport without getting killed first.

"Do you have a safe house?" Ryan asked.

Sure I did. A rogue didn't survive long without one. But damn it, I didn't want to take him there. Alya, yes. Ryan with her? A definite no. But with no other choice, I gave the address to the cabby.

Alya stirred at the sound of my voice and peeked at me over her shoulder. Something about her was so pained it made my heart race. Did she remember? Did she forgive me? No, whatever she'd remembered wasn't the memory I'd been dreading. Couldn't be.

Ryan frowned at me, as if asking me what the hell was going on. I couldn't tell him. Our friendship, our brotherhood, had all but ended the night I'd gone rogue. But to admit that I'd been betraying the Firm for *years* before that… I couldn't. Not even now after he'd taken a step out on a limb to protect Alya.

Not even when it was clear she meant more to him than he'd let on. I turned away. Seeing her with him hurt too much. I wanted nothing more than to steal her out of his arms and hold her. She'd nearly undone me when she pressed her face to my neck the way she always did when we'd made love.

Fuck, I couldn't go thinking about our doomed past now. I slapped at my coat pocket. The pack of cigarettes was there. I'd light up the moment I could. Anything to get back to the Nick I'd transformed myself into. Nikolai Tyrov was dead. Dead. Dead. I was Nick Parker. Former agent with the FBI, borderline dead-beat, serial dater without hope of redemption.

The cab came to a stop in front of my brownstone mansion.

Ryan whistled. "Nice digs."

I shrugged. "Had some money and nothing to do with it."

A beeper went off and Ryan winced. He slipped the beeper out of his pocket. "Forgot to throw this out." He glanced at the screen, then sagged into his seat. "Multi-vehicle school bus accident. Damn." His arms tightened about Alya. "They're calling in all available doctors. Haven't done this since the crash. But I can't—"

She hushed him by placing her hand over his mouth. "Do they need you?"

150

"Yes, but you—"

"Go. I'll be fine. Just, be careful."

He nodded and kissed her wrist. "Listen to Nick, okay?"

"Okay."

After a moment's hesitation, she kissed him tenderly.

It felt like a stab to the gut. I slammed out of the car and marched up to the gate, opening it for Alya. The car drove off, its purr fading in the distance. She moved up next to me.

"Nick."

"Don't," I snapped and stalked to the house. I needed a smoke. I needed to get away from her for a while. It took me the short trip to the front door to realize I'd never escape her. She haunted me, defined my very existence.

She didn't even know. In a tragic way, it was hilarious. I had to laugh. Instead I marched into the kitchen and turned on the stove. I used the flames to light up, inhaling deeply. Alya came into the kitchen. I watched her through the flames, transfixed, remembering the last time I saw her before meeting her again in the hospital. That time she'd been enraged. This time, she was vulnerable. Her shoulders hunched as she hugged her arms.

"I'm so sorry," she whispered. "That time with Luc—"

"Don't." Fuck no. Not this. "It was long ago." My heart clenched, but I covered it up by focusing on my smoking. Deep breaths. One slow, tortured death for me. The way I deserved.

"I would have told him I loved someone else."

Of all the things she could have said, that one brought me crumbling downIn the time it took me to exhale, I dropped my cigarette and stormed across the room. When I got to her, I grabbed her and slammed her body to mine, crashing my lips to hers.

It was like the dreams tormenting me whenever she wasn't with me. Her body melted to mine, arms entwined about my neck. A soft sigh fanned my famished lips, driving me on. I dove my tongue into her mouth for a fuller taste, groaning with relief. The soft hum she released in turn beckoned me. Her fingers tangled in my hair, tugging far from gently. She was thirsting for me too. Craving me.

God, yes.

My hands slid up under her shirt, reveling in the feel of her skin. It was as smooth and supple as I remembered. But then my fingertips found a scar on her back, a few inches above her hip. What would possess her to allow her perfect skin to bear a scar?

I groaned and ripped myself away from her. Too much had happened. A whole century I wasn't a part of. I didn't even know if she'd forgiven me. She keened, her beautiful eyes glazed in confusion. Her chest rose and fell hard and fast.

"Oh my God," she whispered, her voice high. "What am I doing?" She sobbed, hugging herself before turning away from me.

"Fuck." I closed my eyes and tilted my head up. I needed to escape. Needed to gather my thoughts and figure out what to do, because she'd destroyed me all over again. I'd let her, yes. Let her see she still held a terrible power over me, the one thing I needed to hide. Not just that, but I wanted her to. Above all I was still that guy who'd given his heart to her and who wanted to tear it out of her when he saw her with someone else.

It was the thing with her. She was my poison, but I didn't feel alive unless I was drinking her to my own destruction. I stood there, waiting for her to say something, anything. All I heard were my raging breaths and thundering heartbeat.

When I opened my eyes to face her, she wasn't there. Being the fool I was, I immediately went in search of her. I found her huddled in the corner of my sitting room, crying.

Long ago, I'd had this stupid dream that she'd be here, loving the beautiful art nouveau glass work, the stunning furniture. But dust now obscured the light and ghostly white covers hid the furniture. I sighed and knelt next to her. Even though I knew I was setting myself up for a ton of pain, I pulled her to me again, cupping the back of her head. Tears dripped onto my shoulder.

"Y-you'll never forgive me, will you?"

The question shook me to the core so badly that I didn't think straight. "*I love you, Poison. You could never do something needing forgiveness.*"

"*I hurt you,*" she said in Russian, bringing home the fact that I'd just spoken it without realizing. "*I remember. And now I hurt Ryan. What sort of person am I?*"

What could I say? That what she did to me was nowhere close to the pain I'd inflicted in return? Or even the destruction Ryan had cut across her people for centuries? If I told her the truth... No. I couldn't stand to lose her again, so I did the cowardly thing. I picked her up and carried her up to the room I'd once imagined sharing with her.

It needed airing out. I set her down gently and opened

the windows, then occupied myself with removing the dust covers from the furniture. The wood still gleamed. Nothing exactly matched. I'd bought them all one at a time, thinking she'd like each little thing I added for some reason.

She drifted away and dropped onto the bed, curling up. Even though she tried to be quiet, I could still hear her crying. I sat down next to her and she met my gaze. Confusion and pain mingled on her face, making me ache to ease them away. But what could I do?

"You're confused, Alya," I said, trying to fit together words that would make her feel better without throwing myself under the bus. "I didn't help you just now, kissing you." I was supposed to add 'when what we had is gone,' but the words wouldn't leave my mouth. "I'm sorry," I whispered.

She wiped at her eyes. "I hate this."

"I know. Try to rest a bit. You'll feel better."

Alya gave me a small smile watered down with tears. She took my hand and held it while she drifted off to sleep.

"I love you too," she mumbled drowsily, snuggling closer.

I watched over her, wishing with all I was that I'd let Ryan delay me on the morning I'd found her with Luc.

RYAN

The hospital was in a state of absolute pandemonium when I arrived. Everywhere around me nurses, doctors, and frantic parents ran about. Children, many more than I would have thought fit into a bus, whimpered and cried from cubicles. I glanced around and found Dr. Hartley clutching a clipboard and shouting over the noise at an intern. I went over.

"What happened?" I asked as soon as the intern left to do Dr. Hartley's bidding.

She seemed utterly lost, staring at the clipboard as if it held the answer. "I don't know. Five buses were attacked on the way to their schools."

Five? "Attacked? How?"

She met my gaze, giving me a good show of the fear she was trying to hide. "I don't know. The kids keep saying a man threw them off the road, but that's impossible."

I tilted myself onto my heels to keep from reeling. The rebel griffons had to be responsible. "Yeah," I managed, frowning. "Impossible. Listen, I'm going to report to the desk and get my patient list. Call me if you need anything."

"Okay." She smiled half-heartedly. "Good luck."

"Same to you." I walked away, trying to get a feel of

griffon activity in the city. The power I sensed brought me to a stop. I hadn't sensed out so many griffons in one place in years. Now, it felt odd. Foreign. I balled my hands into fists and kept walking. The main desk was awash in activity, serving as the HQ during the emergency. Only one man in a hoodie remained motionless, leaning against a nearby wall, watching.

A buzz of recognition twisted in my stomach and I cast out my power to sense him. Nothing extraordinary, except I could feel four griffs in short range, all on high alert. Just fucking marvelous. I went to get my caseload, trying not to appear aware of the man's gaze following me as I moved.

"ER is full, but as soon as you're needed, we'll call you, Dr. Ryan."

I nodded and picked up my stack of files. I paged through them. All children. All shaken and lacerated. Lots of stitches for me to do.

"Blake," my father said right next to me.

I suppressed a groan and peered beneath the hood. His blue eyes were softer than usual. Must have been the morphine he took. "The underground look suits you. Makes you look like a college guy."

Which was true. Though he didn't seem much older than I did, in reality he had about five centuries on me.

"*I want to talk to you,*" he said, switching to Old Norse. Even in this chaos, it drew a young nurse's attention. I walked away, needing distance. Of course, my father disregarded this completely and fell in step with me. "*I'm not angry at you, but I do think you're insane to shack up with the likes of her.*"

I halted and turned on him, narrowing my eyes. My

father was strong, but my former love of hunting meant I could take him any day, any time. "*I'm not going to talk about this.*"

"*You're going to have to, boy. I'm protecting you both. Niko, too.*"

I lifted my eyebrows. "*Really? So the veiled threats—*"

"*I didn't mean to threaten you, but I can see how you would have taken my words as such.*" He glanced off into the distance. "*However, now that I know where you are, I'm sure you realize that I could have spared a few griffs to take all of you out.*"

He had a point.

"*Except it wouldn't have been to your advantage,*" I pointed out.

He shrugged, tilting his head slightly. "*Come back to the Firm, son. Not because I'm threatening you, but because it's your place.*"

Was it, though? The politics, the jealousy, the bloodshed, and for what? It took some time to get used to living without those things, but now I had tasted freedom, I didn't want to get tied up in all that again. On top of everything, Ali could never be a part of my life if I went back to becoming a monster.

My father sensed my hesitance. "*Look, don't decide anything now. Let's clear out the rebels and then talk, okay?*"

"*Fine,*" I said, my body tensing. Trust him to try taking the gentle approach when it was too late to salvage anything. I had needed this when I was much younger, but not anymore. Now it just muddled things. I turned away and left him behind without looking back.

I'd done it very easily a few decades ago. Cut off any hope of ever having an emotional bond with him.

Physically walking away now was actually much easier. The distance helped me focus.

The intercom called my name, saving me from further aggravation. Family history was impossible. Blood and lives in my hands. I could handle that with ease.

NICK

Alya grew restless in her sleep. Fool that I was, I lay down next to her and held her. I never wanted to let her go. For her sake, I would have to. This trust she had in me wouldn't remain once she remembered. I wouldn't betray her again, wouldn't take advantage of her vulnerability. She deserved that much and more. So much more.

Alya whimpered, burrowing her face against my chest. I could only smile, gently stroking her hair the way she loved. I missed this.

Too soon, Ryan's power made itself felt. He was coming in fast. I grimaced and started to extricate myself. Now was a bad time for me to face his questions. I was almost free of Alya's hold when Vince walked in on us, freezing when he saw what I was doing.

His eyebrows shot up. "I thought she's Ryan's girl."

"She's no one's girl."

His disbelieving expression didn't improve my mood. "And yet, I get the idea Ryan'd be seriously pissed if he saw you right now."

"Saw what?" Ryan asked, walking towards us.

Damn. Damn. Damn, damn, *damn*. I looked at Alya, but couldn't bring myself to wake her. It was too late now anyway.

Sure enough, Ryan's jealousy and rage rolled over me

in waves. "What's this?"

I frowned at him. "Not what you think. She had nightmares." True enough, but then, I'd just gone and underestimated Ryan's power.

His eyes dulled as they gazed at Alya. "Want to leave her be so we can talk?"

Now he was just pissing me off. But let go I did. I stood up and went to the living room, shoving my shoulder against his on my way out.

Vince joined me a second later. "You know, for a chick I've yet to see awake, she sure is stirring up a shitload of trouble."

"Fuck you."

He smirked. "Don't for a second think I'm not sympathetic. Your love life has nothing on mine."

Ryan closed the door behind him before coming to stand by us. "I don't care what your history with her might be," he said quietly, glaring at me, "but she's not yours to play with any more."

"I know that, but neither is she yours. Once she remembers what happened with Luc Davenport, she'll kill you as much as look at you."

A muscle by Ryan's temple ticked, the only indication of my jab hitting home. "Our father showed up at the hospital. Juiced. He's personally offering us our old places in the firm."

"Does he know about Alya?" I asked, amazed.

The muscle ticked again. "Yes. In fact, he made it quite clear that he's protecting us all."

"For now," Vince inserted. Both of us frowned at him. "Come on, I'm as likely to get killed as you two. Shot the griff and the Davenport guy. I'm pretty sure I deserve a say."

"True," Ryan said, turning his frown at me. "Vince has a point. We've broken Firm rules left and right since the plane crash. If we put the Firm back in power…"

"We might as well be signing our death warrants," I completed, "but what choice do we have? Align with the rebels? Go to the protectors? Cut and run?"

"And then what? Stand by, watching humanity go to hell? Or get killed for nothing? Because I assure you, unless Ali remembers and helps us get into safe contact with the protectors, Davenport will kill us on sight."

"Not to mention the fact that the Firm will *definitely* want you dead if you pick any of the other options," Vince stated. Another excellent point to the vamp.

"Besides," I said, glancing at the closed door of Alya's room. "When she remembers, she won't want anything to do with us."

"You," Ryan corrected, staring me down.

"What?"

"You." He repeated. "She forgave me during World War Two. Saved my life, even. It's why I became a doctor. And why I've risked everything to keep her safe." He walked towards her room, and stopped with his hand against the door. "She forgave me and gave me a second chance. For that alone, I'll love her until the day I die. The way I see it, our only option is to wait for her to fully recover her memory and then see her safely home. After that, we help the Firm. That's my plan. Are you with me?"

"Yeah," Vince said. "I want to die."

I was too floored to speak. She forgave Ryan? *Him?* But she had continued to hate me. And why wouldn't she?

Ryan went in and shut the door.

I returned to the kitchen and lit up another cigarette. Fuck it. It shouldn't have mattered anyway. Not when we were both sure to die.

And yet, it did.

ALERIA

In 1898, I was back in France, and the whole time I kept a subconscious eye out for Luc. Paris was his assignment, but if he was here, I saw no sign of it.

My group of protectors never bumped into his, which was pretty rare given how strong our targets were. Fact was, he'd been avoiding me since the day I told him I was in love with someone else. Of course, he'd never made the leap to thinking of Niko as my beloved, but he resented me nonetheless. I wished he didn't. I missed him, missed our moments of being able to talk about everything and nothing.

But I couldn't worry about that now. We were on patrol, me and my group. We rested against the *Opéra Garnier's* dome, throwing our senses out wide, searching for any griffon close to our wards. I didn't believe in hunting them. Only in defending our people. Some protectors differed from me and burned for the griffons' destruction, but I made sure to keep those types out of my group. Couldn't be at odds with my companions the whole time.

Tonight was eerily quiet. As if the griffs had left the city. I shivered, glancing at the protectors at my sides. All of them wore unsettled frowns. I wasn't the only one feeling as if something was wrong.

Griffons almost never left a place unless they went rogue, were ordered to move, or were summoned into a pack. Since both the former scenarios were unlikely, the latter stood out as the most plausible explanation. A pack of griffs was never a pleasure to deal with.

"We need to find them right now," I said, trying to veil my unease in steady tones.

"And our other group," someone said to my left.

True. The more protectors we had, the more powerful we were.

"Fire up," I ordered and closed my eyes, drawing in the flames from the nearby gaslights.

The others followed my example, taking in fire wherever they found it. The air around us went dark, and blackness circled out from our location as we drew in more and more power. The advantage to this was two-fold; the griffons couldn't spot us in the darkness, but with fire glowing inside of us, we'd be able to see them.

I was the first one to find a sign that something was seriously wrong. A single flame, flickering as if someone tried to draw its power but failed. It was in Montmartre. I burst into a run, knowing the others would follow. The light might have been nothing—gaslights weren't always reliable—but something told me to get to that light and fast.

We found Montmartre in darkness and the first corpse on the steps of the *Sacré-Cœur*. He was a protector. A new one I didn't really know.

All of his powers were drained.

One of my party cried out the outrage we all felt, but I hushed him, instead focusing on finding the rest of the fallen protector's group. Now that we were closer, we should have found them with ease. Instead, I only sensed one protector in a sea of griffons. Luc.

With a pained cry, I ran forward, drawing in as much power as I could muster, pulling from and giving to my own group. The bastards had drained about six other protectors of life, so they'd be even more powerful than before. They had to be powerful in themselves, to be able to attack a group of protectors with impunity.

I couldn't allow myself to care. Not when we needed to save Luc. Besides, those other six protectors couldn't be saved. We could no longer sense them. There was too little life left to salvage.

We found him in a small square, weakened by the numerous draws on his power. My chest clenched with panic and I lit up, killing the first griffon I found. There were about twenty of them and the power they exuded was staggering.

We knew we could die tonight. Still, we fought. For our drained comrades and for the one who'd managed to stay standing. We punched and kicked and lit them ablaze, but the griffs were too many. Their draws overcame our every attempt at gaining power.

A small church off to the side kept catching my attention. There, in the deep, shadowed doorway stood two griffs. Their power was unrivaled. I could feel them buffeting against my defenses and those of my group, not really trying to force their way in but making us aware of their presence. Their power made the air about us crackle. If they started killing, there would be no defense.

Recognition clenched around my heart.

"Aleria!" Luc groaned, staggering towards me. "*Run.*"

I looked into his eyes for the briefest of moments,

wanting to tell him I'd never leave without him, but then he dropped like stone, his life snuffed out in an instant.

Seeing him fall cut out the last remains of my heart. I screamed in pain as his loss consumed my soul.

"Fuck!" one of the men in my group shouted. "The Reaper's come!" And with a soft groan he was gone.

My blood went ice-cold.

"Fall back!" I shouted. I had to get my group away before the Reaper killed them all. One-on-one I could take him, but he wasn't alone, and he'd use that to his deadly advantage.

"Fall back where?" one of my protectors shouted, right before she was cut down.

Gasping for breath, I did a quick turnaround, looking for a gap in the circle of griffons around us. There wasn't one.

We were as good as dead. There was nothing to do but try and pull my broken soul back together and fight my way out. Exhaustion crept up my body, making it ache while the griffons continued to draw out my energy.

I felt out the weakest spot in their trap and went for it, killing as many of them as possible, as fast as possible. Every moment passed with a weakening of my power. My group's lives went out one by one. The Reaper was worked with ruthless ease, almost lazily as if killing for power bored him.

And I…I was failing my people.

Finally, I bashed open a hole in the griffon trap, but when I turned back to call my group, they were all gone. Every single one was hollowed out, their faces contorted in fear and pain. No! Releasing a raw scream, I went for the Reaper. The griffons grabbed me, drawing out the last of my fire. My knees buckled as I sobbed.

"Stop," the Reaper ordered and stepped out of the shadows. The dark-haired monster from my nightmares. Ryan. His green eyes gleamed with hunger. "She's ours."

No one argued with him. They didn't dare.

His companion in death came to stand next to him. It was Nikolai, wearing an expression of pure hatred.

RYAN

Ali slept restlessly. Her brows furrowed as she tossed her head one way and the other. Whatever she was dreaming wasn't good. Her eyes quivered beneath her lids. Maybe I should have woken her up, but it didn't feel right. Instead, I held onto her as she tensed and trembled, wishing with all my heart I could shield her from her memories.

I ran my fingers through her hair, whispering softly to comfort her. It didn't help much.

She woke up with a sob and opened her eyes. Her eyes dulled with deep anger. Hatred flooded over the bridge between our souls.

I recoiled, panic stealing my air. I knew. She remembered the night we'd killed Luc Davenport, and I'd miscalculated by assuming she'd be okay once she did. Her rage burned me like hot daggers. She pressed her hands against my chest, pushing us apart.

"Ali…"

"Don't even open your mouth," she whispered. She might as well have shouted for the impact it had on me. Aleria jumped out of bed and backed away when I followed, watching me warily. "I trusted you."

My heart sank. "No. It's not like that, Ali. You forgave me." I willed her to understand, but she shook her head.

"Forgave you? I wanted to *kill* you. Both of you. Did you enjoy having me in your hold for so long? God," she wailed, "I gave myself to you!"

I rushed her and pulled her into my arms. "Ali please. You have to listen to me."

"No!" she shouted, shoving at me with all her might. I felt her reaching out, searching for power, opening herself more and more.

"Stop it!" I shouted back, stepping towards her, but within seconds her hands lit up.

Nick burst into the room, but halted when he saw Ali. "Oh God." He made to move towards her, but she hit him with a blast of heat that sent him staggering back.

Ali sobbed. "*You* killed him. Because you were too stupid to just listen to me when I tried to explain."

"I know!" Nick tried again, but her ever growing power kept him at a distance.

The air around her flickered with the intense heat spreading out around her.

"Ali please," I begged. If she wanted to kill me, that was fine, but not like this. Not without her remembering the whole thing. "You still don't know everything."

"Right," she scoffed, "and I'm just going to go on believing you like an idiot." One of the furniture covers combusted. "My whole life, I had one true friend. You took him away from me! And for what?"

"Revenge," Nick said, hanging his head. "It hurt me so much to lose you that I wanted to return the favor. I was stupid, Alya."

"We both were," I said, wishing to make her understand. "We were empty shells of pure hunger, nothing more. Life was nothing but endless battles of survival and death. Meaningless. So meaningless."

"Until you," Nick murmured. His words hit me like an axe to the chest. I felt his pain, his longing for her. He'd sense the same coming from me. Right then, it hurt too much to speak, so I nodded my agreement.

For a moment, she relented, wiping at tears flooding down her cheeks. Nick and I just stared, hoping for some clue as to what she'd allow us to do next.

A gunshot shattered our unstable peace. Ali gasped, narrowing her eyes at us while flames licked along her arms. "You've done it again! Well done. Caught me."

"What?" I asked, then went cold.

Griffons. At least thirty of them. Upstarts to power players, they were all moving in.

Nick moaned. "Alya, this is you. You let them see you."

She shook her head and backed away from us, letting her fire run along her shoulders. It'd kill us to go near her.

"Guys!" Vince shouted from somewhere else in the house. "We're in big trouble."

Seconds later, windows and doors shattered and the staircase thundered under a legion of heavy footsteps. Another gunshot went off somewhere above us. Within seconds, some upstarts crashed through the door. Ali was the first of us to react, picking off griffons with morbid abandon as they came through, as if she didn't care that there was no hope for survival if she didn't escape.

"Run!" I shouted at her, letting as much of my true nature free as I dared. I was honed to kill, but I wouldn't kill her. Anyone out to harm her, on the other hand, I drained in seconds, kicking and hitting to get to Ali. I needed to talk sense into her, but her rage and power kept me at bay. The griffons who tried to approach dropped dead in seconds. Still, I could sense the draws the older ones put on her. They didn't try to take too much at a time. They were smart enough to let the upstarts distract her while they siphoned off her life force bit by bit. At the speed they were going, she wouldn't even notice until it was too late.

I went for them, hoping to God I could drain them before they realized I was the threat they should have neutralized first. More came in, as powerful as Nick or Alick, and they all went for my power.

Their draws went through me with enough force to drop me to my knees while I clung to my life force. I cast out my most powerful draw in return. My thoughts swam, but my true nature was exhilarated at a chance to gain more power. But I was weakening too fast. I collapsed in a heap.

Some griffs carried Vince in and pinned him down, preparing to kill him. I distantly felt Nick struggling against death as well, and a surge or regret washed over me. We used to be brothers and best friends. All that had disappeared when I had refused to understand that he'd done the right thing to leave.

Ali's life force flickered to oblivion even as she continued fighting. I loved her, and she'd die hating me.

More power crowded in on me, and a dozen of the most powerful Firm members stormed in, wearing hoodies to cover their faces. I knew my father was there, though. The draws lessened somewhat, but griffons kept flooding into the house, pulling at my soul and threatening to tear it asunder. I lost touch with my surroundings, instead listening to my heart beating slower and slower.

172

ALERIA

I wanted to die. Luc had been killed because of me. It had been my fault, and I hadn't been able to stop it. It was only fair that I died the same way. Maybe it would somehow make up for his loss in some way. Maybe. I couldn't be sure.

I couldn't trust myself, not after I'd betrayed the protectors yet again. How could I trust the monsters who'd haunted my nightmares?

So I fought.

I grabbed the nearest griffon and snapped his neck, then glanced at five upstarts trying to gain hold of my life. With a mere thought from me, fire licked up their bodies as if someone had doused them in kerosene. Apparently the upstarts realized they were way out of their depth, and they stopped coming. I cast out my senses, seeking out the strongest draws in the room. The griffs wielding them stood off to the side, biding their chance to kill me.

The room buzzed with energy. I sensed the battle being waged between some of the most powerful griffons, Ryan and Nick.

Nick dropped to his knees first. He was still alive, but he wouldn't be for long. Ryan fell moments later.

The bastards were targeting each other. I didn't dwell on it. I threw the hottest fireball I could make at one of the big players, killing him instantly. The remaining big players turned on me. A flood of power drew on my life. If I could only take them out, my death would at least count as a form of vengeance for Luc. I charged at them, ignoring the sensation of my life being torn to pieces. As long as it was in me, I'd spend it killing as many of the griffons as possible.

More and more of them came in, stretching my soul even further, but I slammed into my target, kicking him hard enough to send him flying into a wall. Next, I rammed one's nose into his brain. One came up behind me and I rewarded him for it with a fatal punch to the throat. I blasted another with heat until his insides blistered.

The whole time, other griffons leeched my energy out of me. I kept coaxing myself to kill. One more.

One more.

One more.

I stopped noticing or caring how I did it, just that each successive kill came slower and slower as my fire waned.

More and more griffons joined the fray. Instead of killing me fast, the new arrivals merely used my power to augment their own. They turned on those who came first, fighting each other and, slowly but surely, draining me.

My fire was about to give out when it rushed back into me in full force. My body sagged as I took the brunt of the energy. There could only be one cause for this. A protector was foolish enough to use some of his power to kindle the dying spark in my soul to life. It gave me enough strength to light an inferno in the room and then, as if I'd summoned them, the protectors were there. Over fifty of them.

They released a blood-curdling battle-cry as they sprinted into the battle. They were absolutely ruthless, killing any griffon who dared to put a draw on us. They targeted the griffons with deadly accuracy, lighting some on fire, decapitating others with silver-edged swords.

"Leave them, griffons of the Firm!" one of the griffons shouted. At the command, some of the most powerful griffons there stopped and backed away, surrounding Ryan and Nick. Not one of them dared to place another draw on us.

"Ali!" someone shouted and I followed the sound with my gaze, finding five upstarts working to tear a vampire limb-from-limb. I threw fireballs at them without a second thought, aiming for any draw I could sense, but being careful to avoid striking the vamp. He shot to Nick's side.

It seemed to signal that the tide had turned. More than half the living griffons retreated. I prepared to follow, but a hand on my shoulder restrained me. I turned, preparing to order the protector to work. Instead, I found the one phoenix who outranked me.

My father. With a raw sob of joy, I threw my arms around him, closing my eyes to savor the love I felt as he held me. "I thought you were dead!"

He squeezed me. "Couldn't…not without you." Three words were left unsaid, but I knew what they were. *To take over.*

"Mum?"

"She was so tired, darling."

Memories of my mother's soft touches and soothing voice flitted back in a million fragments. My throat burned with hot tears I couldn't show. "I'm so sorry I didn't make it in time."

"Oh, darling, we thought you were dead. It was so much worse than thinking you missed another death ceremony."

Maybe my father's words were true, but my sense of loss numbed me anyway.

"Come on. Davenport, make sure she gets home," he said, beckoning Armand to approach.

Armand…

I couldn't face Luc's twin. Not while the memory of Luc's death was so fresh. Instead, I followed my father's gaze to where it rested on Nick and Ryan, both watching me in anguish.

"Milord," Armand said, sounding peeved. "The griffons—"

"Will live to fight another day," my father stated. "As soon as I thank the two who kept my daughter alive."

I forced myself to look at Armand. The sight of him gave me a remorseful pang. I instinctively knew it wasn't the first time.

Armand's jaw clenched, but no one dared to contradict our chieftain.

I didn't say anything, either. What could I say? I hadn't died as penance, so my betrayal stood, and coming out with the truth would destroy us. The hatred ran too deep. After everything I'd learnt and experienced, there was only one sensible thing to do.

I nudged Armand's arm and walked away, knowing he'd follow with his group. I felt pain both from Nick and Ryan before I shielded my power, becoming invisible to their griffon senses at the same time.

"It was you at the hotel, wasn't it?" I asked, glancing

towards Armand.

"Yes," he clipped, then gave a pointed look towards the group.

His tense posture and the ticking muscle in his cheek told me to shut up. He was so similar to Luc, but so different. Armand and I had never gotten along. This I also instinctively felt. I faced forward once more and nursed my heart. The stupid thing had gone and broken again.

RYAN

Ali left without even a glance back. Every step she took tore out my heart a little bit more. After she disappeared from sight, I sat up and let my head hang forward. I'd gotten so used to having her with me that losing her felt like the griffons had succeeded at drawing out my soul. I glanced toward Nick, who was still lying on the floor, eyes squeezed shut. His pain mirrored mine. Idly, almost moving on their own, his hands drifted up and patted his jacket.

"Are you okay?" I recognized my father's voice, but felt almost nothing. A mere twinge of resentment. Of course I wasn't fucking okay.

Someone cleared their throat, drawing everyone's attention. His eyes shone with some sort of secret. *Aleria's eyes.* The ache eating at my insides came back for round two.

I fought it back by letting my attention drift away from him to the huge pack of protectors around him. They were tense, powered up and waiting for one of us to make a wrong move. Worse, they chose *not* to hide the fact that they were ready for the kill, but their wariness made sense.

The battle had taken a severe toll on both griffon factions. With the full benefit of surprise, the protectors had fought through the battle with most of their number intact. I only felt two fiery life forces fading, but even those seemed to be bolstered by the others. No wonder they were so bold.

"I thank you for guarding over my daughter," the Chieftain said, snaring my gaze once more. "She is precious to me. To us."

I merely nodded. Much as I wanted to point out that this was about more than earning the protectors' favor, I knew the wise course was to shut up. The Chieftain would definitely be able to sense the roaring flood of feelings going through me at the mere mention of her, but he didn't know our relationship had gone beyond what he assumed. It would stay that way. The least I could do for Ali was to let her live the life she knew and trusted without complication.

The Chieftain smiled gently. "Are you a Firm man?"

"They both are," my father inserted, sparing me the discomfort of having to search for a diplomatic and safe answer. He tossed his hood back, revealing his shoulder-length golden locks and blue eyes. Dressed as he was, he looked like a grown-up skater boy. Only the highest ranking members of the Firm knew the powerhouse ex-Viking lurking beneath the exterior.

The Chieftain burst out laughing. "Tyr. It's been some time."

My jaw dropped. I'd thought only three griffons alive knew his Norse name. Him, me and Nick.

"Still as discrete as a fool, I see." My father went to him, face somber.

The Chieftain shrugged. "Why bother? Everyone with any sense can figure out who and what you are." He

179

glanced at the corpses strewn throughout the room. "Having problems, I see."

My father's anger flared at the finely pointed insult. And shame. He hadn't wanted the Chieftain to see this, his greatest failure.

"Yes," my father said, jaw clenched.

The smile faded from the Chieftain's face. "I see." He sighed heavily and rubbed at his jaw. "Will it be all out war, then?"

"Yes."

"I see."

The protectors tensed as one. Some of them scowled at the ceiling.

"Get lighters," the Chieftain commanded.

Nick breathed soft laughter and pulled a cigarette from his pocket. A moment later, he lit it and inhaled. The Chieftain watched, entranced by Nick's blatant disregard for his own health. So did my father, his whole face slackened with surprise.

"What?" Nick demanded, blowing smoke out through his nostrils. "This *is* my house." He looked around the charring remains and another stab of his pain went through me. "What's left of it."

The Chieftain turned back to my father, gave him a nod, then left. The rest of his guards followed him out in silence. My father didn't show any outward signs of relief, but I could sense how much effort he put into mastering his emotions. I was probably the only griffon strong enough to experience this, though. With the Firm—and the whole world—tilting at the brink of disaster, those loyal to the Firm needed a strong leader.

My father focused on me. For the first time in my

eternal life, I saw him vulnerable. He refused to show it, but it was still there, lurking beneath the surface. That was new. Part of me had always assumed my father was partially hewn of stone.

"I need you to take your place as Vice President," he said and walked out, disregarding the shocked stares coming from the rest of us. Typical of him, he didn't wait for me to say yes or no. He simply assumed I'd fall in with his wishes.

And damn him, he was right.

NICK

Me and Vince sat in Romano's apartment, waiting for him to come home. I itched for a smoke, but since Romano had quit, I couldn't smoke inside without him kicking my ass. I'd get a drag when I was away from here and on my way to the Firm's New York HQ.

"Never thought I'd help out some griffs," Vince said.

"Me neither, bud. Me neither."

"How are you doing?" he asked after a moment.

"I'll live." I actually felt like crap. Losing Alya again felt like a kick to the chest. Even if I never technically had her this time. "What's keeping Romano?" I asked, aiming the subject off of Alya.

Vince shrugged. "Probably following up some sort of lead."

Moments later someone fidgeted with the lock and the door opened. Romano came walking in, carrying a *Carnevale* mask. A buzz shot through me. It was *my* mask, the one I'd kept at my desk.

Romano paused for a moment before recognizing us. "Breaking and entering now?"

I sank back into his sofa, smiling. "Lifestyle of the infamous outlaw. Can I have the mask back?"

"Sure. I managed to sneak it off before my new partner swooped onto your desk for evidence. Always seemed to mean a lot to you."

"Yeah," I said.

He handed the mask over. "What's with it, anyway? Looks real old."

"Italian Renaissance," I said and carefully laid it on my arm rest.

Vince whistled. "You must be real attached to it."

I was. Alya had worn it the first time we met without trying to kill each other. "So. How's the partner?"

Romano grimaced. "I'll have my hands full. Not only is she a tenacious little fire-cracker, but Righetti doesn't seem to believe a single word I'm saying to lead her off your scent."

"Righetti?" Vince repeated, sounding tense. "As in Sylvia Righetti?"

"You know her?" Romano asked, frowning.

"Shit. Yeah, I know her. She's in the NSA's paranormal division."

"What?" Romano and I both shouted back.

I shook my head to clear it. The NSA had a paranormal division? "How do you know?"

"She's been on my back for some time to go find out where New York's Arch Vamp is."

"What the fuck is she doing in the FBI, then?" Romano demanded.

"Assessing paranormal risk," Vince said, making air quotes with his fingers. "I don't think they know about griffs and phoenixes, but if one of them ever does find out, bet your ass that it'll be Righetti."

I scowled. Trust mortal bureaucracy to be an extra annoyance in this whole war. "Then I guess you better talk to her, Vince. Give her false information or something."

"No fucking way I go near her. She'll shoot me between the eyes. *with* a silver bullet."

"What?" I asked. "I thought she needed your help."

"Let's just say my 'help' led her to a demotion. And she's one *very* career orientated lady. No. No thank you."

Romano sighed and swiped his hand down his face. "Great. I guess I'll have to find a way to keep her off the trail. Short of killing her, I mean."

"Sorry, man," I said. "I'd offer to help, but that would be complicated. In the meantime, I'd better go. Wouldn't want her to track me down in your apartment. Meet me in Central Park next time."

"Okay," he said. "I'll keep you posted."

"Thanks. See ya." I tucked the mask into my jacket before heading for the door.

Vince patted Romano's shoulder farewell and followed me. Once we were out of sight of any mortals, we shot over to Firm HQ.

The whole time we ran, my thoughts wandered back to Alya. To that night in Montmartre, when I'd destroyed what we'd had. When the moment of truth had come, I couldn't go through with watching her die.

I had convinced Ryan to let her go so she could regain her power. After all, I'd reasoned, she wasn't worth all this effort if most of her life force had already been leeched out. It had worked, but my act of mercy had only enraged her, and she had promised us she'd hunt us down.

Now she probably hated us even more for lying to her.

I arrived at headquarters and lit up a smoke at the front door. Vince caught up just as I took my first drag.

He scowled. "Those things'll slowly kill you."

Yeah, I knew that when I started. But there were only two options for penance of what I'd done: an excruciating, slow death or my true love killing me. Nothing else.

ALERIA

I sat in a bay window in my father's peaceful, airy sitting room, watching rain coming down over New York City. The mansion was huge, like the home in London I vaguely remembered. Something was missing, though. Maybe it was my mother. No, that couldn't be it. Although I loved her, I was used to her absence.

She hadn't been a protector, so her life cycle had been much shorter than mine. Maybe that was why she didn't really feature in my memories. She took up such a small part of my life, but I had loved her. My heart ached every time I remembered her beautiful smile in Regency London.

Armand strode into the room, shaking his hair like a wet dog. He stilled when he caught sight of me. "Not sleeping, then?"

Truth was I hadn't slept at all. Not for days. The whole time it felt like more memories were around the corner, lurking just barely out of reach. I needed a break. To recover from the pain my most recent memories had brought me.

To my surprise, Armand hadn't moved. I seemed to recall that his conversations with me were always perfunctory at best. But was it true? Could I really trust myself after my disastrous mistake with the two griffons?

My memories and instincts had already failed me when I'd trusted them most.

"No," I said, frowning at him. That was the most annoying thing about this. I was at a complete disadvantage towards everyone I knew. Yes, I recognized them. Sometimes I even had a sense of what the association had been like. I just had no idea what my interactions with them had actually been. All I had to go on were tiny fragments of memories that didn't add up to the whole.

Armand's inscrutable expression left me without any clues, so I took the safest route and turned my attention back to the cityscape.

He ventured closer and cleared his throat.

So the awkwardness was to continue. Luc had always been the one who smoothed things over between Armand and me. The realization squeezed my heart so hard I pressed my hand against my chest in an attempt to dull the pain.

"Why do you think they didn't kill you?" he asked.

"I don't know," I said. I didn't, not really, and *that* was killing me. There was so much I didn't know. Would I have acted differently if I did? Was the information so important?

I couldn't drive away the feeling that I'd made a horrible mistake. Ryan had become a doctor in the time since my last memory. Nick became a cop. They had completely immersed themselves in humanity, so the image of them as the monsters who'd killed Luc just didn't fit them. But why did they lie to me?

Armand sat down next to me, leaning against the window. As casual as his pose seemed, I couldn't imagine he was comfortable. Still, he'd made an effort. I needed to, as well.

"I'm sorry about Luc," I said, even if my words could never even begin to cover the shallowest of my feelings on the matter.

"Yeah," he said after a moment. "Me too."

I crossed my arms and hugged myself, glancing out of the window. "Do you hate me for not saving him?"

He should have hated me. Luc was basically dead because of me. If I'd stayed away from Nick all those years ago, Luc would still be alive. I couldn't remember everything about his death, but of this I was sure.

"I don't know," Armand said and released a heavy sigh. "Did you try?"

Those three words burned me. "Of course I did! How could you even ask that? I loved him."

"And yet, you turned him down again and again."

"Wouldn't you?" I asked forcing myself to meet his gaze. Armand and my father were the only protectors I knew of with life cycles as long as mine. "Knowing someone you loved would be reborn without you? That they'd live whole lives you can't share?"

He clenched his jaw. "I wouldn't. Not if the brief moments our lives intersected were worth it."

I flinched. He was right. I'd risked everything for Nick once, presumably because my love for him had been enough to make the risk worthwhile. Only, I'd never guessed what the cost would be.

The truth was I didn't remember. I knew I loved Luc, but…if there had been no Nick, or if Luc had survived, would we have been married? Would we have had a happy life even today? Would I have felt whole?

I didn't know.

Before I could explore my feelings any further, my father walked in. His brown hair was graying at the temples. The wrinkles he had only added to his good looks, making him appear distinguished.

"My girl," he said and bent down. His kiss to my forehead flooded me with love, bringing to mind the million times he'd done it before.

I gave him a hug in return, savoring his warmth and strength. "Please don't go," I said impulsively, squeezing my father tighter. I'd only just found him again. The thought of him dying and never coming back terrified me.

He petted my hair. "I won't. Not just yet."

"Milord?" Armand asked.

My father stepped back. "We are to help the Firm regain control of the griffons."

"Why? Let them destroy themselves. I'll even go help them over the brink."

My father frowned at Armand, and he averted his gaze. Few people had the guts to stand up to their Chieftain. "What say you, darling?"

I looked up at him. "I don't know what to say." Once again, my memories stirred, but they stubbornly remained out of reach.

My father's expression softened. He cupped my face between his hands. "Griffons protect humanity the same way we do. The fight we have with them is between us only. Mortals shouldn't suffer for our choices. Do you agree?"

His voice was so gentle, so patient, so loving. Tears stung the back of my eyes. I nodded. "And the Firm being destroyed would have a bad effect?"

He smiled. "Indeed."

Armand scowled. "Fine. We help them, but so help me, the Reaper and his brother will die before I'm done with them." With that, he stalked out of the room, leaving us both staring at his back.

My father sighed. "Sometimes, I think he's too angry for his own good."

"We can't blame him," I said. "Half his soul died with Luc." My voice cracked.

"Yes," my father said, "but there is such a thing as forgiveness."

His words reverberated in my mind until they thundered, taking me back to a night in the Battle of Britain.

ALERIA

Bombs rained down on London, coming closer with every passing second. I needed their fire—desperately—but they weren't coming fast enough. The Reaper sprinted right behind me, his draw battering at my defenses while I frantically searched for fire. There wasn't any available while people waited out the bombings. Only the fire exploding from the bombs themselves would save me now.

If the bombs didn't blast me to smithereens first.

Damn the Reaper for finding me in my WAF uniform, and damn society for still expecting us to wear heels with skirts. I kicked my shoes off while I ran, relieved when doing so let me pick up speed.

I darted across the street to a few buildings that had survived the previous bombings. I needed to hide. The first bomber flew over just as I sprinted into an alley. A few steps later, I heard the Reaper's victorious laugh. He grabbed hold of my arm and slammed me into a wall.

This was it. I was as good as dead.

His draw pushed against my defenses. *No.* I ripped my left hand from his grasp and sucker punched him. He staggered back a step, but before I could escape, a bomb dropped nearby. The blast flattened us both. I landed on top of him. I had a brief glimpse of the Reaper's horrified expression before pain blanked out my vision. My scream mingled with his as tons of brick and mortar drove a metal shaft through our torsos. I couldn't think, couldn't breathe from the anguish. My hands gripped at the front of the monster's shirt as if I sought certainty that he was trapped beneath me.

The bombs thundering down roused me from my stupor. Yes! Fire! Finally, I had my chance to rid the world of this menace. I reached out through the only hole in the debris trapping us. It was excruciating to move, but this was more important than my comfort. Once I killed the Reaper, Luc's death would be avenged and my past actions could finally be redeemed.

The Reaper's breath stalled and I glanced at him. Surely the shaft hadn't killed him? No, but for the first time in my life, I saw his eyes. They were green and dull with pain and fear. I swallowed, but kept drawing in the inferno around us.

As soon as I released the blast, he'd be obliterated and I'd be free.

Except… his eyes.

He threw back his head in an attempt at a pained gasp.

"What are you waiting for?" he demanded. Shudders wracked through his body, shooting pain through me.

I held my breath and squeezed my eyes closed, waiting for the worst of my pain to fade. The fire continued to build in my soul. Its heat comforted me. Soon, it would free me. But when I opened my eyes again, it was his gaze I found first. His breaths were choppy. Sweat beaded his brow. He tried so hard not to look scared, but his eyes were glazed with fear.

Finally I was ready. I had enough fire and energy going

to move a building. I only had to take a deep breath and kill the man I'd most wanted to see dead.

I inhaled, preparing to blast out energy. He shut his eyes and slowly turned his face away. It undid me. This wasn't the way to do this.

No. If I got him while he was defenseless, I'd be no better than the griffons were when they preyed on phoenixes. I'd get him later, when we could have a fair fight.

When I could beat the stuffing out of him myself first. That sounded good, much better than cold-blooded murder.

He blinked his eyes open. His brows knitted together as if he was confused at still being alive.

"Why am I still here?" His voice cracked with pain.

"Because unlike you," I said, "I'm more than a mindless killer."

He winced. "Really? Because you're damn good at it."

His words made me grit my teeth, or maybe it was the horrific pain radiating from my back and abdomen. "But not at being a conscienceless bastard."

The Reaper barked a harsh laugh, shooting pain through us both. We groaned.

"Fine," he said when he caught his breath. "Granted. You deserve to live more than me. So do what you must and get out of here."

"I'll burn you to a crisp."

He met my gaze. "I know."

"I can't."

His eyebrow shot up. "Doubtful."

"Fine. I won't."

"Won't?"

"No."

The Reaper frowned. "Do you realize I wouldn't hesitate if our places were reversed?"

More bombs thundered close by. They wouldn't let up for a while. We'd be stuck together for hours if we survived. I was being stupid. Every second I was above ground put me at risk. Even my powers of regeneration couldn't save me if a bomb blasted me to bits.

"Yes," I said, but a lump formed at the back of my throat. Why couldn't I kill him? This time, I averted my eyes, trying to get a grip on my emotions. I hated this man. He'd killed Luc. He'd tried to kill me multiple times. Now I had him at my mercy for once, and that was exactly what I extended.

A hot tear slipped out of my eye. He wiped it away with a surprisingly gentle touch. "Odds are we both die here if you don't escape."

"Why do you care?" I demanded, then gasped because raising my voice clamped my body in a vise of torture.

"Fucked if I know." His tremulous smile drew a scowl from me.

"You're scared of dying." I said, yanking the proverbial rug out from under him.

"You'd be too if you were headed where I am."

"Oh?"

"There's no redemption for the likes of me," he said with complete finality.

I couldn't help pitying him. What sort of life had he led? A bomb exploded too close for comfort. I whimpered, cowering against his chest despite myself. Sand filtered down onto us. He wrapped his arms around me.

The small act of comfort was enough for me to know I'd made the right decision. "You *are* more than a mindless killer," I whispered, more to myself than anything, but his hold on me tensed.

"No, I'm not. I have no choice about it."

"There's always a choice. And with that choice comes redemption or doom."

"Right." He huffed out a wry laugh, wincing. "Supposing I left and became a good person, I'd be hunted down."

"Really?" I asked, wondering if he'd take the bait. I couldn't tell him I knew opiates disguised griffons from each other. And from protectors, for that matter. Revealing my knowledge would require me explaining my relationship with Niko, and I really didn't want to get into that.

His brows furrowed. "Even if I managed to escape the griffons, I might not stay out of trouble. And then, you'd be there to kill me."

"Me?"

"Yes, you. You hate me, remember?"

It was surprisingly difficult to confirm my feelings when he was hugging me to his chest. More tremors shook the earth, filtering dust onto us. He rubbed between my shoulders when I tensed.

"There's such a thing as forgiveness," I said, frowning at the idea and at myself for suggesting it. Could I really forgive the man who'd killed my best friend? Let alone the countless others he'd killed over the centuries.

He snorted. "You couldn't forgive me."

I sighed, resting my forehead to his chest. "Don't you just get tired of it all?" Because suddenly, I was exhausted.

I didn't want my life to be defined by who I killed and when. There was more to my life than that. Death and killing were necessary parts of being a protector, but what was I protecting by carrying my hatred around? Nothing. It only kept hurting me.

"Yes," he said softly, gasping when another bomb exploded nearby. "I am tired of it."

"I mean," I said, "I don't even know your name...only Ryan...but I know you use your last name."

"To us, you're the Chieftain's daughter, or *her*." We shared a breathy laugh.

To Niko, I'd been Alya and Poison. I was hit for the thousandth time by the huge loss I'd suffered when he'd left. He was one of a kind. "I'm Aleria."

"Blake Ryan." This time, our gazes held. "If I walked away from all this and became a better person, would you be able to forgive me?"

There it was. The big question. If I said yes, the ramifications for both our lives would be huge. The very idea went beyond all my training as a protector.

Yet...I wanted to say yes. I wanted to be free of the darkness that had ruled me even before Luc had died. And as insane as it sounded, I wanted to free this tortured being from his self-created prison.

Seeing him as not all that different made me crave peace. Without forgiveness, true peace could never exist.

I swallowed, then nodded.

I woke up with a gasp, pressing my hand to the scar I'd kept as a reminder of that day.

Oh God. I'd made a huge mistake.
I had to find Ryan.

Acknowledgements

As always, the first and foremost thank you must go to my Heavenly Father, who's given me my love of stories and the tenacity to see them finished.

Then, thanks to my family, who put up with me slinking away to write at every opportunity

And of course, this book wouldn't be here if not for the help of these fine individuals: Murees, Connie, Randi, Shell, Vikki, M.J. and Caitlin.

Last but not least, I just want to say a quick thank you to you, dear reader. If you're reading this, you're one of the awesome people who are helping me write more books. That makes you an amazing person in my opinion. I'm honored that you'd take the time to read what I've written. Thank you.

GET IN TOUCH

If you'd like some news on *Endless* or just to see what Misha's up to at the moment, you can find her on these social networks:

Tumblr
mishagerrick.tumblr.com

Twitter
@MGerrick1

Google Plus
+MGerrick

You can also mail her at mishagerrick@gmail.com.